TANGLED EMOTIONS

AN ARRANGED MARRIAGE SAGA

SHIRISHA S. PATI

Made with ♥ on the Notion Press Platform
www.notionpress.com

Dedicated to my Best Friend - Lipsita. This one's for you, Lippi!

Contents

Foreword *vii*

Preface *ix*

Acknowledgements *xi*

Prologue *xiii*

THE UNSPOKEN VOWS

1. The Proposition 3
2. A Reflection 7
3. The Engagement 11
4. Insta-Connect 17
5. Echos Of Yesterday 22
6. Stepping Closer 27
7. Twirling Hearts 33
8. Wedding Jitters 37
9. The D-Day 41
10. Veiled In Vermilion, Blinded By Vengeance 45

TURNING TIDES

11. Shattered Dreams 53
12. The Battle Of Egos 58
13. Perfect Couple 62
14. Long Road Ahead 67
15. Calculations And Cracks 71
16. Avni In Trouble 75
17. Hope For Tomorrow 80
18. The Gift 85
19. Whispers In The Hallways 89
20. The Nighmare 97
21. Blast From The Past 102
22. The Reunion Party 108

Contents

23. Beyond The Shadows 112

24. The Unveiling 117

ASHES OF YESTERDAY, SPARKS OF TOMORROW

25. Love And Loath 123

26. The Bitter Truth 127

27. The Reckoning 131

28. Seeing Through The Hate 134

29. A Bloom In The Desert 138

30. Bridges Burned? 142

31. The Cost Of Indifference 147

32. The Revelation 151

33. Shattered Illusions 155

34. Distance And Decisions 160

35. The Weight Of Repentance 164

36. A Glimmer In The Grey 168

37. The Hunt 174

38. Tangled Emotions 178

39. A Bridge Across The Chasm? 182

40. Echoes Fade, Promises Bloom 186

Epilogue I 191

Epilogue II 197

Foreword

Having been a professional content writer and having authored several FanFictions and edited or beta-read others, I consider it an honor and privilege to have been entrusted with beta-reading 'Tangled Emotions'. I have beta-read for Shirisha over the span of the years I've known her and I'm struck by how sincere and serious she is about her writing. She is not just proactive about seeking feedback and taking it constructively but also makes a conscious effort to improve and the results are evident for all to see in this book.

Tangled Emotions is about loss and hate, revenge and acceptance but mostly, it's about love. All forms of love - whether it's familial or fraternal, romantic or platonic. It's about letting go and changing yourself, because we all know that as human beings, our most significant trait is our ability to change and to better our own lives.

This book chronicles Aarav and Navya as they navigate the slippery slope of arranged marriage and while doing so, conquer their fears, process their past and come to terms with their future. Let the magic of Shirisha's skillful pen, that beautifully depicts the complex world of these characters, lead you to enjoy this story as much as I have done.

-Riya

Preface

"Tangled Emotions" is a story woven from threads of darkness and light, where loss and hate intertwine with the vibrant hues of love in all its forms. Within these pages, you will encounter characters wrestling with profound grief, consumed by the desire for revenge, yet striving, ultimately, towards acceptance.

But at its core, this is a story about love. The fierce bond between family, the unwavering sacrifices of siblings, the tender vulnerability of romance – all these facets are explored, revealing how love can be both a source of immense pain and an unparalleled force for healing.

This journey is not easy. It is filled with difficult choices, heartbreaking betrayals, and the raw, messy realities of human relationships. Yet, it is a testament to the resilience of the human spirit and our capacity for growth. For as we navigate the complexities of life, we discover that our most remarkable trait is our ability to change, to learn from our mistakes, and to rise from the ashes of our past.

"Tangled Emotions" invites you to explore the depths of human experience, to confront the darkness within ourselves and find the light that guides us forward. It is a reminder that even in the face of overwhelming adversity, love, acceptance, and the courage to change can lead us towards a brighter future, one where we can finally, truly, begin to heal.

Acknowledgements

The journey of writing this novel has been a long and winding one, and I wouldn't have reached the end without the support of some incredible people.

First and foremost, I want to thank my parents for their unwavering belief in me and my dreams. Your encouragement and love have been a constant source of strength. To my siblings, thank you for always being there to listen, and for generally making life more interesting.

Thank you to my best friend for life - Lipsita. You couldn't be a part of this book, but I know you always their to cheer for me.

A special thank you goes to my friends, Shibani and Riya. Your sharp eyes and honest feedback during the proofreading process were invaluable. Thank you for catching the inconsistencies and typos that somehow slipped past me – you've made this book immeasurably better.

Finally, I am deeply grateful to Notionpress for giving this story a home.

Prologue

Navya Oberoi - now Singhania sat on the edge of the bed, her heart beating fast with a mix of excitement and nervousness. The room was beautifully decorated, a reflection of the care and attention her new family had put into making her feel welcome. She had spent the past few months preparing for this moment, imagining what it would be like to start a new life with Aarav.

She glanced at the ornate mirror, her reflection a strange mix of unfamiliar finery and quiet apprehension. The kohl outlined her eyes, making them appear larger. She barely recognised the woman staring back, a woman adorned in hues of red and gold, a woman who was now a wife.

A wave of nervousness washed over her, leaving her stomach in a knot. What would her life be like? Would they have things to talk about? She had hoped that this journey would be beautiful, where they could build a life together, filled with if not love, but respect.

She had always been independent and strong-willed, and she wondered how those traits would fit into her new role as a wife.

Aarav finally entered the room, and Navya's heart skipped a beat. But as she looked into his eyes, she saw a storm of emotions that she couldn't quite place. There was anger, but also something else—pain, perhaps, or frustration. She felt a sudden urge to reach out to him, to understand what was troubling him, but before she could, he spoke.

"Don't," he said, his voice laced with venom. "Just ... don't."

Navya's brow furrowed. This wasn't the welcome she had expected. She swallowed, trying to quell her rising panic.

"Aarav, is something wrong?"

Without another word, Aarav moved with a deliberate stiffness, like a puppet controlled by unseen strings. He tossed his wedding turban onto a nearby chair and began to walk towards the balcony.

"Aarav," she held his arm, making him face her. "What happened?"

Aarav moved closer, his presence suddenly overwhelming, filling the small space between them. He leaned in, his voice dropped to a menacing whisper.

"Let me make one thing perfectly clear. Don't ever try to assert your right to be my wife," he took her hands off his arm.

His words cut through Navya like shards of ice. She felt a tear escape, tracing a lonely path down her cheek. Her voice trembled as she spoke.

"But... but why? What did I do?"

"You exist. That's your crime. And believe me, Navya, I will make your life a living hell. You are now at my mercy and there is no escape for you," Aarav said, his voice cold and devoid of any emotion.

THE UNSPOKEN VOWS

ONE

The Proposition

The scent of wet clay and graphite filled the room, a familiar comfort to Aarav Singhania. He traced the delicate lines of a proposed concert hall, his brow furrowed in concentration. The design was intricate, demanding precision, a stark contrast to the chaotic whirlwind of emotions he kept firmly locked away.

"Aarav!" He heard his cousin Megha call him and instantly groaned looking up from his file. He wanted to complete the project and head back home soon and here he was being disturbed.

"You don't need to yell all the time, I am not deaf! And how many times have I told you not to disturb me when I am in office?" He frowned only to see her grinning from ear to ear.

He knew that grin, something crazy was going on, in that equally crazy mind of hers.

"Guess what?" she said, completely ignoring his irritated look and continued grinning.

"What?" He sounded indifferent and continued his work as he tried to remain nonchalant.

Megha snatched away his file and banged it on his table. She gave him a death glare making him stand up from his chair.

"I know you are a very busy person, Mr. Architect but better take out some time to hear from your sister and best friend!"

Aarav and Megha had grown up together. Aarav was four months older than Megha and they were best friends. They were inseparable, they had gone to the same school, and the same college. They had the same gang of friends; they had even hated the same teacher. If you didn't know them personally, you would think that they were twins and not cousins, they were that close.

Aarav pushed his drawing board aside with a sigh, running a hand through his perpetually dishevelled hair.

"It had better be important, Megha. You know I don't like distractions."

Megha pretended not to notice the subtle barb. She knew him too well.

"Speaking of distractions," she began, her tone becoming dangerously sweet, "I have a wonderful proposition for you."

Aarav's heart sank. He knew that tone. It was the tone that preceded disaster.

"Let me guess," he said, his voice flat. "You have found another candidate for my marital bliss?"

Megha beamed, completely unfazed by his cynicism.

"You're perceptive as always! This girl, Aarav, is incredibly intelligent, beautiful and...,"

"Not interested!" he said dismissively, and picked up his pencil again.

Megha was the one who had pushed him towards Samaira. With all the constant teasing, Aarav had realised his feelings for Samaira. But reality had been a bitter pill to swallow. Samaira, it had turned out, had eyes for someone else.

Megha had been so blinded by her desire to see Aarav happy that she hadn't considered the possibility of rejection, the possibility of someone else's heart being involved. Her well-intentioned meddling had backfired spectacularly, leaving a trail of hurt in its wake. The worst part was that Aarav was too tender to place any blame on her and that made her feel much worse.

She now carried the weight of her mistake, a constant reminder of her flawed judgment. She wished she could rewind time, take back her meddling.

Drowned in guilt, she has been trying to find the perfect girl for her brother since then.

"At least listen to me once."

Aarav groaned, resting his head in his hands.

"Megha, we've been over this. I am perfectly happy as I am. I don't need a life partner, I need... Well, I need more time to finish this concert hall."

"But Aarav," Megha persisted, pulling out a chair and settling down opposite him, her voice laced with genuine concern. "It's been six years! You can't keep living in the past. You deserve happiness, a family, someone to share your life with. Not just blueprints and construction schedules."

He looked up, his eyes tinged with a sadness she knew all too well.

"Marriage isn't a puzzle to be solved, Megha. It's not something you just slot into your life, like a missing piece. And honestly, Aarav and marriage are like antonyms for me."

"Hey, don't say that!" she hit him lightly, her usual cheerful demeanor replaced with a resolute firmness. "At least meet her. For me. Just one dinner, no pressure. If you don't like her, fine, we'll never speak of it again."

He hesitated, his gaze flitting back to the half-finished design. The idea of meeting a stranger, of going through the awkward charade of pleasantries, felt like a monumental task. The thought of opening himself up again, even superficially, was terrifying.

Yet, he knew Megha wouldn't let the issue drop. She was stubborn, and more importantly, she genuinely cared. He saw the worry etched on her face, the genuine desire for his happiness.

"Fine," he finally conceded, his voice heavy with resignation. "But you know I am still not over that heartbreak.

"I know and I understand. Trust me, I think you both need each other."

"Why do you think so?" Aarav asked not understanding where she was getting into.

"Navya has also had her heart broken."

Navya Oberoi frowned as she walked out of her room. Her mother, Anjali, was perched on the edge of the plush velvet sofa, her eyes sparkling with an almost unnatural enthusiasm. Her father, Rajesh, sat opposite, pretending to be immersed in a copy of the Economic Times while his ears were clearly tuned into their exchange. Kavya, Navya's younger sister, was perched on the armrest, a mischievous glint in her eyes.

"Navya," Anjali began, her voice a honeyed purr, "Look at this profile, he is a successful entrepreneur and an archite..." she trailed off.

Navya, perched on the armchair, ran a hand through her loose braid, her gaze fixed on the intricate embroidery of the throw cushion. The mention of "successful entrepreneur" sent a familiar shiver of unease down her spine. The last "successful entrepreneur" she had been involved with had left her emotionally drained and financially lighter. The memory of that man, his charming smile and smoothly delivered lies, was still a raw ache in her heart.

"Maa," Navya sighed, her tone laced with weariness, "I am not in a hurry to get married."

"Not in a hurry?" Kavya piped up, her voice teasing. "Dee, you're twenty-eight! You're practically ancient in our family. Remember how Maa says women are only really prime candidates for marriage until...well, until..." she trailed off, pretending to forget the exact age, eliciting a groan from Navya.

"Don't be silly, Kavya," Rajesh finally intervened, lowering his newspaper slightly. "Your sister has a point. It's her life, and she should decide when she's ready. But," he added, quickly adding a caveat when Anjali's eyebrow arched, "it wouldn't hurt to just...meet the young man. No pressure, just a casual conversation."

Navya knew that 'casual conversation' in her family's lexicon translated to a thorough interrogation and a detailed report on her compatibility with every aspect of the man's life.

"Dad, I am completely focused on my work. The new collection is launching next month, and I have to oversee everything. I hardly have time to sleep, let alone date."

"That's another thing," Anjali said, rising and pacing the room. "You need to slow down. You're overworking yourself. Marriage would be good for you, it would give you the stability and companionship you need-"

Stability. She had thought she had stability once, and this is where that had landed her. She loved her fashion design business, "NK Designs," it was her passion, her sanctuary, and she couldn't imagine sharing her life with someone who didn't understand her work and her drive.

"Mom, you're making it sound like I am a broken machine in need of repair. I'm fine. I just..." she paused, trying to find the words, "I need time."

Kavya, sensing an opening, leaned closer.

"What the hell is wrong with you? It's been a year for god's sake!"

Navya sighed, giving Kavya a withering glare. Even her sister, usually her ally, had been recruited into the "Get Navya Married" brigade.

"You know I am still not..."

"I know everything," Kavya said, fed up. "And I also know that Aarav Singhania is a good man."

Navya sighed and looked at her younger sister. She had made a decision in the past and regretted it. She was left heartbroken. This time, she decided to trust her parents' decision. Maybe, it was finally the time to move on.

"Fine," she said finally, her voice low and resolute. "I'll meet him. But on my terms."

PPP

TWO

A Reflection

The soft jazz playing in the background of "The Cozy Corner Cafe" did little to soothe the anxious flutter in Navya's stomach. She had ordered tea, a beverage she hoped would project a picture of calm and composed femininity. The truth, however, was that her palms were clammy, and she'd already checked her reflection in the window three times in the last five minutes. Her meticulously chosen beige kurta felt suddenly too simple, and the delicate silver earrings she'd decided on seemed inadequate.

Nervousness spread all through her body, leading her to continuously tap her legs as she glanced at the watch.

He was late. Thirty minutes late, to be precise. Her carefully constructed mental image of a well-mannered, punctual man was crumbling a little faster with each passing tick of the clock. Her parents' enthusiastic description of Aarav Singhania – kind and successful - had painted a picture of someone far more considerate than this.

Each chime of the little bell above the door sent a jolt of anticipation through her. Some were groups of friends, some were couples, and some were just people grabbing a quick coffee. None of them were him. She re-read her mother's text message one last time:

"Remember, be yourself. He is a nice man."

Easy for her mother to say, she wasn't the one sitting here feeling increasingly self-conscious.

Finally, the bell chimed again, and this time he entered. He was tall, and she recognised him instantly from the photograph her parents had shown her. Aarav. He wore a fitted black t-shirt, dark jeans, and his hair was slightly tousled as though he had just run a hand through it. He scanned the room, and his gaze landed on her. He walked towards her table, not with a smile of apology or even a nod of acknowledgment, but with a kind of distracted air.

"Miss Navya Oberoi?" he said, his voice was a little flat, as he stopped opposite her.

"Aarav Singhania," he introduced himself after she nodded.

He immediately pulled out the chair and plopped down.

Not a single word of apology. No explanation. He didn't even look directly at her. Navya felt a spark of annoyance ignite in her chest. So much for first impressions.

The traffic has to be blamed," Aarav said as if reading her mind. "And, I didn't come alone. I have brought back-up."

Navya raised an eyebrow, a hint of skepticism creeping back into her mood. This was getting more bizarre by the minute.

Two figures emerged from behind Aarav; one a young man, just an inch shorter than Aarav. The other, a girl, a teenager really, with bright, observant eyes and a shy smile that peeked from beneath a curtain of dark hair.

"This is my younger brother, Aryan, and my sister, Avni."

They all settled down as they placed their orders.

20 minutes passed by and all they had been doing was sipping coffee. No one uttered a word except for placing their orders. Aryan fidgeted with his phone, his gaze fixed on its screen rather than the elegant woman they were meant to be impressing. Avni, on the other hand, stared at Navya with a mixture of awe and shyness, her hands clasped tightly in her lap. Navya had been waiting for Aarav to say something, but on seeing him sitting quietly for so long, she had finally built up the courage to start the conversation.

"I am Navya, I am a fashion designer."

Aarav looked up in surprise. He didn't know that.

"That's... That's great. I am an architect."

"I know."

He just nodded not knowing what to say next.

"I was talking to them by the way," she said pointing at the boy and girl who just looked at her silently.

"Hello Aryan, Hello Avni," Navya flashed her best smile

"Hello, I'm studying in class 9th," Avni smiled back, sipping her hot chocolate.

"That's nice. And you?" Navya asked Aryan.

"I am in my 2nd year of Commerce," He replied.

"NK Designs are yours right?" Avni asked.

"Yes."

A smile spread across Avni's face.

"Oh my god! I just love your designs! You are great! I..."

She squealed in excitement but stopped realising that her brothers were looking at her, amused.

She smiled at Navya and got back to sip her drink.

The conversation flowed easily after that, Navya adeptly navigating the initial awkwardness. They talked about random things. Aarav, meanwhile, watched the interaction with growing surprise. He had expected his siblings to be quiet and reserved, he wasn't sure how they would take an addition in the family. Instead, they were engaged, even a little animated. He had never seen Avni open up so quickly to a stranger. And Aryan, who was usually so cynical, was actually smiling and engaging in a genuine conversation.

He looked at Navya, her eyes twinkling as she listened intently to Avni, who was now excitedly describing a dress she had always dreamed of designing. He couldn't help but smile. Maybe this whole arranged marriage thing wouldn't be so bad after all.

"Can you guys wait in the car for a few minutes?" Aarav said to his siblings. "I would like to have a talk with Miss Oberoi alone."

Both of them nodded. Aryan smiled at Navya in affirmation and Avni waved a bye to Navya who waved back.

"Miss Oberoi, I want you to know that Aryan and Avni are my biggest responsibilities. After our parents' death, I am all they have. And if things work out between us, they will be your priorities too. I don't want to force them on anyone. But as my life partner, you would have to accept them."

"Mr. Singhania," Navya sighed. "I would love to take care of them. But before we make any decision, I want to tell you about... my... I... I was in love with someone but he... he cheated on me with... with someone I knew. I have been single since then. I don't know what you will decide but I don't think I am at that stage of life where I can love anyone else."

She said all that without looking at him. She kept avoiding his gaze.

"Same is my case," Aarav stated, gaining her attention. "I did love someone a lot but never dared to confess to her. She considered me just a friend so I have no one to blame. But to be frank with you, I don't even want to get married at this stage in my life."

"Isn't it ironic that we both don't want to get married but are still sitting here and discussing our fate ahead?"

Aarav just looked at her thoughtfully.

"Why did you agree to meet me, Mr. Singhania?"

"Because of Megha," he shook his head remembering all the blackmailing his sister had done to send him.

Navya chuckled. Directly or indirectly, Megha had tried to play a matchmaker. Her cousin Shanaya, at whose wedding Navya met her, were close friends. She and her cousin, Shanaya were close friends. Shanaya had told her everything about Navya's heartbreak when Megha had gone to Navya's parents with the proposal. She had known Megha for years and really liked her

"Ms. Oberoi?" she heard Aarav calling her.

Damn! God knows for how long he had been trying to call her!

"Where were you lost?"

"Ah, nothing. Just thinking about Megha. She is trying to play cupid," Navya chuckled again.

Aarav smiled faintly, agreeing with her.

"And yes, she had already told me what you just said," Aarav said. "She thinks we both can understand each other because we both are on the same page."

"What do you think about it?"

"Honestly, I just trust Megha. She would make the best decision for me, for Aryan and Avni. For all of us."

"I have made decisions for myself and regretted it. I know my parents would do the best for me, so here I am."

"I just want you to know that I am still not over her."

Navya just nodded. She was not over him either.

THREE

THE ENGAGEMENT

Aarav's heart beat rapidly as he got ready for the most important event of his life till today. He stared at his outfit, the intricate gold embroidery a stark contrast to the turmoil churning inside him. It was a beautiful garment, no doubt, the kind he would never normally wear. Megha, bless her enthusiastic heart, had insisted on it.

"You can't wear just anything to your engagement!" she had declared, her eyes sparkling with the vicarious thrill of planning her brother's life.

He ran a hand through his hair, the carefully styled strands immediately springing out of place. He looked tired, he realized. The kind of tiredness that came not from lack of sleep, but from the mental marathon he had been running since Megha had dropped the engagement bombshell. One week. One measly week. That's all it had taken for his life to veer so drastically. He was getting engaged to Navya.

He glanced at the clock on his bedside table. 7:45 PM. Just one more hour until they would begin the rituals. One hour until he would place a ring on the finger of a woman he barely knew, and commit, in front of family and friends and the watchful gods, to a future he hadn't even imagined a month ago.

The gentle knock on the door jolted him back to reality.

"Aarav, are you ready? We need to leave in a few minutes," Megha's voice called out, laced with an excited tremor.

He took a deep breath, forcing himself to smooth out the wrinkles in his kurta. He ran his hands down the silk, feeling the weight of it, both literally and metaphorically.

He just hoped, that somewhere within the confines of tradition and expectation, he could find a way to be himself, and find a way to build something real with Navya.

He opened the door, forcing a smile for his sister.

"Yes, Megha," he said, his voice a little tight. "I am ready."

Navya sat in front of the mirror, staring at the reflection in front of her, unable to recognize the person staring back. The beautiful gown adorned her figure, while her make-up was done by professionals.

She grabbed handfuls of the gown, and she gingerly got up, trying not to trip with the weight of the gown. It was heavy.

Walking further away from the mirror, she glanced back at her reflection.

This was not how she had imagined her life to be. She had so many dreams to marry the man of her choice. But now she found herself dressed up for a man she hardly knew. They had met only once. He didn't ask many questions, she didn't talk too much. But that one meeting had made things clear to them - this was going to be a marriage of convenience, neither of them was looking for love.

They both knew, *they would never be able to fall in love again.*

As the priest chanted some mantras, Aarav and Navya stood next to each other, nervous. It's been fifteen minutes since they were standing together but they didn't talk to each other. They hadn't said a word to each other than the brief nod Aarav had given her before the ceremony began.

Aarav looked at the girl who stood beside him. The only thing he knew about her was her name, and that she was a Fashion Designer. Other than that, what did he know? Neither did she know anything about him. She didn't even know what he was experiencing at the moment. He couldn't explain this strange feeling to anyone. Not even Megha. Was this decision correct? He took a deep breath, deciding not to stress too much about it. Aryan and Avni liked her, *wasn't that enough?*

Navya looked at the man standing beside her. Was she doing right? Was this the best decision for her right now? To get engaged to a man she hardly knew? And did he know her? He didn't even know about her profession when they met. She had doubts, and *her doubts were making everything feel so wrong.* She felt a tap on her shoulder and brushed her thoughts aside. She looked up at her mother and realized that the priest had been offering her the ring.

Aarav forwarded his hand and Navya slid the ring on his finger with a sheepish smile, Aarav did the same. But after sliding the ring, he didn't leave her hand. Instead, he interlocked his fingers with hers. Navya looked at him shocked, he was looking at her with a smile. He blinked at her as if trying to comfort her. She looked at their hands, suddenly it felt perfect to her. *Two imperfect pieces, fitting perfectly with each other.* She held his hand more tightly. They both sat down and then he gazed towards the guests who were clapping for them. But Navya kept looking at him, unable to digest the fact that she was committed to him now.

"Where are you lost?" Megha shook her.

"It's nothing. I was feeling nervous and scared a few moments ago, but now I feel overwhelmed. I can't even express what I am feeling right now."

"Relax," Megha assured. "I have read about wedding jitters in books. Could be that. I am sure Aarav must be experiencing the same thing."

Navya looked at Aarav. He was watching Avni and her friends' dance performance while holding her hand.

"Look at him all you want today," Megha teased. "He's going away anyway for two days."

"Going? Where?" Navya asked.

"Bangalore. Don't you guys talk?" Megha frowned and then her eyes widened as realization dawned on her.

Navya's smile faltered. It was true. After their first meeting, she and Aarav hadn't had a proper conversation. Not in person, not on the phone, not at all. It was...uncomfortable. She had chalked it up to the whirlwind of the engagement festivities, but Megha's question brought the odd silence into sharp focus.

"We have been busy," she said lamely, picking at a loose thread on her dupatta.

"Oh My God!" Megha almost screamed, gaining Aarav's attention.

"Why are you shouting?" he asked, annoyed. He was really enjoying the song the girls were performing.

"You guys don't talk! Have you not talked since day one? Do you know anything about each other except your names? Do you even know what the other person is doing?"

"Stop hyperventilating," Aarav rolled his eyes. "You know how busy I am and she is also working. We don't get time."

"Don't get the time? Aarav, you have to take time from your busy schedules for each other. You are going to be a part of each other's lives now," Megha tried to explain in a calmer tone.

"We don't have each other's numbers," Finally Navya spoke and looked at Megha, embarrassed.

Megha shook her head at them. Seems like she would have to sprinkle her cupid magic again. She deftly navigated Navya's phone.

"I have saved his number. Wake him up at 6 AM. He has a meeting at 8 AM and then has to leave for Bangalore by 11," she said as she handed Navya the phone back. "Okay bye."

Navya took the phone, the newly registered contact a stark white beacon on her screen. She nodded absently, a whirlwind of thoughts churning inside her. She and Aarav were about to embark on a life together. She looked at their entangled hands again. Maybe Megha was right, it was just the anxiety before the engagement they talked about. Right now, she was feeling content.

Navya's heart beat rapidly as she heard the ring on the other side. After a lot of hesitation and nervousness, she had finally decided to call Aarav. First, she didn't want him to get late for the meeting. And second, since the time she had received his number, she couldn't wait to talk to him.

Rring, Rring.

Aarav groaned, burrowing deeper into his pillow, hoping the sound would simply vanish. But it persisted, a relentless melody that clawed its way into his consciousness. With a sigh that bordered on a growl, Aarav finally reached out, his hand blindly fumbling for the device on his nightstand. He managed to grab it and, without even bothering to open his eyes, swiped the green button.

"Hello?" he mumbled, his voice thick with sleep. He could barely hear himself, let alone the person on the other end.

Navya chuckled hearing his agitated voice.

"Will someone speak now?" Aarav said irked as there was no reply from the other side. "Who's this?"

"It's Navya."

Aarav's eyes snapped open, the sudden burst of alertness making his head throb.

Navya? Why was Navya calling at... he squinted at the glowing numbers on his phone – *5:50 AM?*

"Is everything Okay?" he asked, sitting up abruptly, the movement sending a wave of dizziness through him.

"Everything is fine," Navya smiled. "Megha had told me to wake you up at 6 AM. You have an important meeting at 8 AM and then have to leave for Bangalore by 11 AM."

"Oh, yeah. Thanks. I am awake now," Aarav said, relieved. Then he smiled. *She would be waking him up every day after marriage.*

"Okay, I guess you should get ready then," Navya said, out of words. "I hope you have packed."

"Yes, I already did my packing last night."

"Cool. I'll hang up then."

"Okay," Aarav said half-heartedly.

"All the best for the meeting."

"Thanks."

"Have a safe journey and take care, Mr. Singhania."

"You take care too Miss Oberoi," Aarav smiled. "See you soon."

'Navya Oberoi'

Aarav typed in the search tab on Instagram.

This was a marriage of convenience for both of them, but Aarav wanted to know about the lady with whom he was supposed to spend his whole life. Stalking Navya's social media account felt like a juvenile idea but it might help him get a few insights into her. Also, it would look silly that he didn't have his fiancee on his friend list if he ever decided to update his relationship status.

A few hundred accounts matched the name. He scrolled through them to find her account. He stopped on an account that had a photo of hers. His hands trembled, and he opened it.

Navya Oberoi

Fashion Designer/explorer/entrepreneur

He read her bio. Her account mostly had pictures of her designs. There were very few personal photos, and the ones there were had her posing with models or celebrities who wore her designs. And he had to admit that her designs were beautiful. She had an aesthetic in her designs that appealed to him.

Navya was going through the notifications on her phone when one caught her attention:

AaravSingham started following you. 1h

FOUR

INSTA-CONNECT

AaravSingham started following you. 1h

AaravSingham?

Navya blinked, then read it again. *AaravSingham.* A giggle bubbled up, starting as a small tremor in her chest and quickly escalating into full-blown laughter. She didn't know why she found it funny. It was just... so dramatically opposite to the man she knew. Aarav was handsome, yes, undeniably so. But he was also the most gentle soul she had ever met. The idea of him envisioning himself as some Bollywood action hero was just... hilarious.

As she opened his profile, she stopped breathing for a moment when she saw his latest post.

He had worn that for their engagement.

Navya opened the post. It was a solo picture of Aarav from their engagement day. She read the caption - ***To new life and new beginnings..!***

She gaped seeing 15603 likes and 4667 comments. They had had a simple engagement ceremony just with family. They were to announce their wedding after Aarav completed his current project. She scrolled down to read the comments. Many had speculated on the occasion already.

OMG! Are you not the most eligible bachelor in town anymore?

No!!!! Why did you have to break my heart?!

Wow! Are you getting married? Why not to me!!

Navya was surprised to see the female fan following he had. She felt good reading the comments. A few girls were sad, and many others congratulated him. It made her feel happy that her fiancé was a sought-after man, but she was surprised to see that there wasn't any reply from Aarav. But she also felt slightly jealous. They were shamelessly gawking at her fiancé, and she didn't like it. Also, why hadn't he made it clear that it was his engagement? Maybe she should wait for Aarav to come back and give her the answers before they announced their wedding. Smiling, she hit the follow button.

Suddenly, an idea struck her mind. She scrolled down her phone's gallery to find a good picture of herself from her engagement day. She loved a candid picture that the photographer had taken of her - she was fixing her earring while smiling at someone. She posted it on Instagram with the caption – To a new life and new beginnings..!

Aarav lay on the bed and checked his Instagram after he was done with his dinner.

Oberoi_Navya06 started following you. 4h

And the first post that was on his newsfeed was Navya's latest post. It was her photo from their engagement day, he smiled reading her caption.

Cool caption, Miss Oberoi! – he sent her a DM.

'Thank you, Mr. Singhania! Caption is shamelessly stolen from the most eligible bachelor in town.'

'Not anymore, I am taken now.'

Navya's heart fluttered. Though they were engaged, it was nice when he made small attempts to remind her that their relationship did mean something to him and it wasn't just a convenient choice. Not getting any reply from her, he texted again.

'Can I call?'

'Yes.'

Her phone rang after a few minutes.

"Hi!"

"Hi, how was your meeting?" Navya asked. Whenever she talked to him, her heart started beating faster.

"Good, how was your day?"

"Like any other day."

"Hmm."

They stayed silent for a few minutes, unable to decide what to talk about.

"Mr. Singhania," Navya said after a while.

"Yes?"

"Why AaravSingham?" She couldn't help asking and then burst out laughing.

Aarav rolled his eyes.

"It's not that funny, Miss Oberoi. It wasn't accepting Aarav Singhania due to whatever reasons, symbols, and stuff also didn't work. So I went to Megha and she put this as a solution. I didn't have a choice."

Navya started laughing again.

"Stop it now," Aarav said, unable to hide his smile. "You can suggest something else if you don't like it."

"No no, it's kinda cool," Navya said and started laughing again.

"Fine, keep laughing," Aarav rolled his eyes again. "Just remember, you're marrying a man who is apparently compared with a lion. You've been warned."

Navya smiled. He could be funny too.

"Mr. Singhania... I was just scrolling through Instagram, and..." she paused, as if unsure how to proceed.

Aarav stretched himself on the bed, a knowing chuckle escaping him.

"And?" he prompted gently.

He knew where this was going.

"And... You have so many followers. In Lakhs!"

Aarav ran a hand through his hair, a slight weariness settling in his eyes. When he designed the great circuit house of the town, he had received lots of appreciation and lakhs of followers online.

"Yes. The social media team does their job well, I guess."

He had lost track of the exact number. It felt less about genuine appreciation and more about the algorithm.

"Not just the team," Navya countered, a hint of pride entering her tone. "You also do a great job. People are genuinely interested in your designs. You're... you're kind of a celebrity architect."

Aarav winced.

"Celebrity is a strong word, Miss Oberoi. I design buildings, that's all. The online world is very different from reality. What you see there isn't the whole picture."

"But... it's a big part of your life, right?" she asked tentatively.

"You know, it's a tool. A way to showcase our work. But it doesn't define who we are. It's a facade, in a way."

"A facade?" Navya echoed, confused.

"I mean, it's a curated version of reality."

"You are right. But do you think the rumours would start because of our posts?" she asked.

"We are announcing in a few weeks anyway. Will it bother you?"

"I don't know. I haven't been talked to by the paparazzi about my personal life, mostly it is just about work."

"Me neither, but I don't think it would affect us professionally in any way. And once we announce our wedding, the news will spread like wildfire and the media will go crazy. Every newspaper and news channel will drive our managers mad with constant calls and messages."

They talked for another few minutes, until there was a comfortable silence but neither of them hung up, neither did they realize when they dozed off, the breaths mingling over the static buzz of the phone.

———

Aarav entered his bedroom at 9 PM, tired from the journey. He picked up the jug to drink water when he realized that it was empty. Leaning against the door he shouted,

"I need water."

He removed his coat and tie when he heard some footsteps.

"Thanks," Aarav said, assuming it to be Robin, their househelp but his eyes widened as he turned around to stare at Navya, who was holding a glass of water.

Aarav blinked. He hadn't expected her. He had assumed it would be one of the house staff, or perhaps his sister. Certainly not Navya.

"When did you... come?" He asked, a hint of surprise in his voice.

She offered a small, hesitant smile, her eyes dipping down to the glass in her hand.

"You said you needed water," she replied softly, her voice like the gentle tinkling of chimes. "I thought... I thought I should bring it."

He took the glass, their fingers brushing for a brief second. It was a fleeting contact, and yet, it sent a strange jolt of awareness through him. He took a long drink, the cool water washing away some of the dryness in his throat.

"Thanks," he said, setting the empty glass on the side table.

Navya just nodded, her eyes still downcast.

"Megha wanted me to surprise you... Are you coming down? All your cousins are here."

"Give me 15 minutes," he said and Navya nodded.

She turned to leave when he called out to her.

"Miss, Oberoi, it's good to see you."

A faint blush crept up her neck, reaching her cheeks.

"Good to see you too, Mr. Singhania," she mumbled, her voice barely audible.

There was a brief, awkward silence after that. Aarav found himself thinking he should say something, ask her about her day, make some kind of conversation. But what felt natural? What wasn't just another rehearsed question from the arranged marriage playbook?

Navya seemed to sense his struggle. She glanced towards the door, then back at him.

"Well," she said, her voice a little stronger now, "We will wait for you downstairs then."

"Okay," he replied.

FIVE

ECHOS OF YESTERDAY

Aarav climbed down the stairs with a smile on his lips. He saw that his family was sitting in the dining room. Rashi, Megha's sister, was busy putting make-up on, his other cousin Kunal was joking with Mohit, Navya's cousin, and much to Aarav's surprise, he was actually laughing at the jokes. Sahil was busy flirting with Kavya while Megha was telling him to shut up. While Aryan laughed at all of them.

Where was Navya?

It was good that she was here. He wouldn't have been able to see her for three more days otherwise. He just returned from a meeting, and he again had to leave tomorrow for a three-day conference in Goa.

He caught Navya's eye across the room, a soft smile playing on her lips as she listened intently to Megha. A wave of warmth washed over him and made his way towards Navya. As he approached, however, he noticed she was no longer looking at Megha. Her gaze was fixed on the far wall, where two large portraits hung.

His breath hitched.

The portrait of his parents.

Navya stood transfixed. He could only imagine what she was thinking, standing there, gazing at the faces of the family she was about to join, a family irrevocably changed by tragedy.

"What are you doing?" Aarav asked as he approached her.

"I was just... Admiring your family," Navya said, her voice hesitant. "These are your parents, right? They seem like wonderful people."

"They were," Aarav sighed. "They were the most wonderful people."

A wave of longing washed over him, so potent it almost stole his breath. He imagined them standing here, beaming at Navya, welcoming her into their family with open arms. He could almost hear his mother fussing over her saree, complimenting her choice of jewelry, asking about her family. He could see his father, ever the pragmatic one, quietly observing her strength and kindness, offering her a nod of approval.

"Shall we join others?" Aarav forced a smile.

As he led the way, he could see the questions lurking in Navya's eyes but he pushed it all down, burying it deep. He wasn't ready.

Navya slowed her pace slightly.

"Mr. Singhania," she began tentatively, her voice low.

"Miss Oberoi, don't," he said, his voice a low, almost imperceptible tremor. "Please. I... I don't want to talk about the accident."

He saw the understanding dawn in her eyes, a flicker of disappointment mixed with a profound sadness. He looked away, unable to meet her gaze.

He knew he was building a wall, shutting her out, but he couldn't help himself. The pain was too raw, the memories too vivid.

"Just...not today. Okay?"

Navya watched him, her heart aching. She wanted to reach out, to comfort him, but she knew, instinctively, that this was a bridge she couldn't cross, *not yet.*

"Okay," she whispered, her voice barely audible. "Not today."

"But I wish you could have met them," Aarav said, the words tumbling out, unguarded.

The weight of the moment pressed down on him, a poignant reminder of what was lost.

"They are a part of you, Mr. Singhania, and through you, I feel like I know them already."

He looked at her, his heart swelling with gratitude. Her words were simple, yet profound, a testament to her empathy and her ability to understand him.

Trying to compose himself, he took a deep breath. He didn't want to burden her with his grief, *not so soon.*

He looked ahead, Megha was looking at them with concerned eyes.

"I think she would like to talk to you," Aarav said and left to join his cousins.

Megha walked towards Navya.

"Aarav and his parents... it's a sensitive topic. He doesn't talk about them, ever," she said in a low voice.

"But why? They clearly meant so much to him."

"He was young when they died. When the accident happened, Aarav was in the car with them... He suffered injuries while they... And it hit him hard, shattered him. He just... shut down after that. He built this wall around himself and he hasn't let anyone in since."

"So he never talks about it? Never grieves?"

"Not that I have ever seen. He's very... uptight about it. Everyone knows to avoid the subject. I tried but I don't want to trigger his bad memories."

Navya absorbed the information, her heart sinking.

She knew it wouldn't be easy, but she wasn't one to shy away from a challenge. Aarav was carrying a heavy burden, and she wanted to help him share the weight. She wanted to bring light into the shadows he had spent so long dwelling in.

"Leave all that," Megha said, her eyes sparking. "How did Aarav react when he saw you today? Was he surprised?"

Navya smiled. Aarav was glad to see her. This was new, this idea of creating a life together. It was thrilling and terrifying all at once, but seeing that soft smile on his face, Navya realized she felt something akin to happiness. It was a realization that soon, everything was going to change. She was going to be Aarav's wife and would take care of him.

"OMG, you are blushing!" Megha exclaimed with a smile on her face interrupting Navya's thoughts.

"Don't start again! I am not blushing. Why would I blush?" Navya answered sternly but failed to hide her blush.

"Oh please, you are blushing because you are thinking about Aarav," Megha said, rolling her eyes.

"Dee is blushing?" Kavya appeared from nowhere and squealed excitement.

"Have you started liking him?"

"Hold it, Kav. We are just getting to know each other. Don't get too excited," Navya said, making Kavya pout.

"So, do you guys talk now, I mean on the phone?" Megha asked, looking keenly at Navya.

"Yes. Thanks to you!" Navya grinned.

"Hello!" Navya looked at a young boy with a mischievous smirk walking towards them. "I am Sahil, your youngest brother-in-law, soon to be."

"Hi," Navya replied with a smile. "You were not there at the engagement?"

"Yeah, I had exams, so couldn't come. Megha Dee planned this get-together so that I could meet you." Navya just smiled in reply.

"So, how do you feel about getting engaged to my brother? The greatest Aarav Singhania, you know, he is a stubborn, arrogant, no-nonsense man," Sahil joked.

Navya laughed, and Aarav looked at Sahil from a distance, he somehow knew that Sahil must be making fun of him.

"I am just kidding, he's not that bad, just a little tough on the outside and soft on the inside," Sahil said. "Like a coconut!"

"He has never shown his stubborn or arrogant side to me," Navya laughed.

"Really?" Sahil scratched his head. "Then is he two-faced?"

Navya chuckled. Sahil was a fun guy.

They joined others at the dining table. Aarav walked and sat opposite Navya. They both looked at each other and then turned their gaze. The image of half-naked Aarav filled Navya's head, and she closed her eyes trying to control her rapid heartbeat.

"Bhai, why don't we plan a family holiday?" Kunal asked. "Let's invite Bhabhi's family too."

"That sounds nice," Megha instantly liked the idea. "I'll talk to my parents. Aarav, what do you think?"

"Since when do you need my permission?"

"If Navya's family is coming then you need to be there too. Just tell me when you can get some free time, for a week at least."

"A week??" Aarav exclaimed in shock. "Meghs, that's too much!"

"Come on. Bhaiya," Sahil said. "Can't you do this much for Bhabhi?"

Both Aarav and Navya looked at each other.

"Say yes, Bhaiya. It'll be fun!" Avni chirped in excitement.

"Yes Aarav, it's been a long time since we went on a holiday, come on." Megha tried to convince him.

"Please say yes, Bhaiya. Please," All of them started requesting in unison.

"Okay, okay fine," He finally gave up.

"You decide when."

"End of this week?" Megha suggested.

"No," Navya said hesitating. "I have a three-day conference this week."

"Where?" Aarav asked, his heart suddenly beating faster.

"In Goa," she replied.

"Conference on Architecture and Fashion," both Aarav and Navya said in unison.

ᑭᑭᑭ

SIX
STEPPING CLOSER

The ambient sounds of chatter and rustling papers filled the air as Aarav and Navya found their seats in a large, well-lit seminar hall. A mix of curious attendees filled the rows before them, each eager to gain insights into blending architecture and fashion for sustainable urban living.

Aarav sat calmly beside Navya, their elbows nearly brushing against each other. The weight of their secret felt like a heavy cloak draped over their shoulders.

Navya fidgeted with her pen, her nails tapping an erratic rhythm against her notepad. Each tap echoed the rapid thumping of her heart. She stole a glance at Aarav, who appeared effortlessly composed, nodding and taking notes as if he were in a mundane meeting. But for Navya, it was electric, intense—anxious with the knowledge that in just a few months, they would be *husband and wife.*

"Mr. Singhania," she whispered, too anxious to keep her voice steady. The sound of her own whispers felt forbidden amid the larger conversation happening around them.

"Yeah?" he replied, tilting his head toward her. He turned to look at her, with a small smile on his face. Her heart fluttered suddenly as her eyes drifted to his lips.

"What if someone finds out?" she asked, her voice a mere tremor. She could feel a flush creeping up her cheeks, a mix of excitement and anxiety.

"Relax, Miss Oberoi. No one will even notice."

Navya bit her lower lip,, her eyes darting toward a group of seminar participants nearby, wariness creeping into her demeanour.

"Looks like this session is going to be interesting. They are discussing how architecture influences fashion and vice versa. I can't wait to see what insights we'll gain." Aarav said as he read the seminar schedule.

"I know right? It's fascinating how our fields overlap. I can't stop thinking about how the environment shapes my designs. The way light falls on fabric, even how the colors of a building can inspire a collection. It's all connected and I had never thought it would," Navya replied excitedly.

Her work was her passion, Aarav concluded to himself with a smile.

As they listened intently to the speaker, Aarav sneaked a glance at Navya's notebook, which was filled with sketches and notes. He noticed the fine details in her designs, the beautiful curves and lines reminiscent of architectural forms.

"Your sketches are amazing," he said as he leaned closely. "The way you play with geometry is similar to how I approach my projects."

"Every line tells a story, and every texture evokes an emotion," she said as she looked at the presenter.

"....We would appreciate it if you guys make pairs of an architect and a designer for the workshop tomorrow," with that the speaker wraps up, and the attendees begin to mingle. Aarav looked at Navya, sensing mutual excitement.

"Want to grab a coffee and talk more about this collaboration?"

"Absolutely!" She grinned. "But are you sure, no one will find out?"

"Relax, no one will notice."

The sun poured through the expansive windows of the spacious studio, illuminating the eclectic collection of sketches, fabric swatches, and architectural models scattered across the large wooden table. Aarav leaned over a scale model of a luxury hotel. The sleek lines and modern design showcased his architectural prowess.

Navya was sorting through a dozen different fabric swatches for a collection that would go with the model.

"Hey, what do you think?" she asked, holding up a bolt of royal blue fabric that shimmered in the sunlight. "I want to create something that channels the royal spirit of the hotel design."

Aarav looked up, momentarily distracted by the way the fabric danced in the light.

"That's beautiful," he replied, his eyes drawn to her enthusiasm. "It would definitely complement the minimalist aesthetic. What about incorporating some architectural elements into your designs? Like angular cuts or asymmetrical lines?"

Navya's eyes sparkled at the suggestion.

"That would be incredible!" She stepped closer, examining the model. "But I think it has to tell a story, Mr. Singhania."

Aarav turned the model slightly to catch the light, inadvertently creating a closer distance between them.

"What kind of story are you thinking about?" He could feel an unspoken energy crackling in the air around them.

Aarav's hand brushed against Navya's as he reached for another sketch pad.

He stiffened as his fingers grazed Navya's. It sent a jolt through him, a sensation he had never anticipated feeling in such a simple act. His heart raced, and a mix of curiosity and uncertainty filled his mind. The sketch pad he reached for suddenly seemed unimportant. Aarav stole a glance at her, wondering if she felt the same flicker of chemistry, grappling with the question of whether this moment could shift their relation of compromise into something deeper.

As Aarav's hand brushed against Navya's, her heart skipped a beat. She glanced at him as her heart raced at fastest pace, unsure if he had felt it too. This was not part of her plan. Their families had orchestrated this union, a wedding planned by others, and yet here they were, sharing an unexpected connection amidst their conference and workshops. She had always imagined their marriage as a practical arrangement, an union of compromise rather than a dance of emotions. But in that second, she could almost see a future painted in vibrant colors, just like they were planning for the model right in front of them.

"What kind of story are you thinking, Miss Oberoi?" he whispered looking into her eyes and stepping closer to her. The soft floral smell of her perfume distracted him momentarily.

"I... That... I... Forgot."

Aarav smiled, he knew this journey was going to take them somewhere, as professionals and as a couple.

He knew that it was a journey that extended beyond blueprints and sketches.

"We have to finish the project ASAP. Before the gala tonight," he said as he snapped out of his reverie. He stepped back and traced his model with his finger, trying to distract himself from his accelerated heartbeat and the intoxicating effect of Navya's perfume.

"I really hope we win," Navya said as she focused on her fabric swatches.

"It's more important to learn than to win," Aarav frowned.

"I like winning," she grinned and he shook his head at her, chuckling.

The dimly lit room pulsed with the rhythm of a soft melody, complementing the whispers and laughter of the guests. Aarav leaned against a marble pillar, nursing a glass of something amber and potent. He pretended to listen to Mr. Singh, the CEO of a rival firm, drone on about market trends, but his mind was elsewhere. He noticed the way Navya held her champagne flute, lightly twirling the stem between her fingers. *A nervous habit?* Or a sign of someone who was used to navigating these social waters? He counted at least three people who approached her in quick succession, each one lingering longer than necessary. She handled them all with grace, a polite smile and an even more polite deflection.

He saw her discreetly brush a stray strand of hair behind her ear, revealing a delicate silver earring shaped like a crescent moon. A small detail, but it struck him as artistic, thoughtful. Something that spoke volumes about her personality, hidden beneath the layers of societal expectation that surrounded them both.

She was working the crowd like a seasoned diplomat, dazzling with her easy smile and sharp wit. He noticed the way she tilted her head when listening intently, the way she subtly steered the conversation to showcase her latest design.

Meanwhile, Navya, after skillfully extracting a potential collaboration opportunity from a well known designing company, caught Aarav's eye across the room. A subtle challenge bloomed within her. She smoothly excused herself, and began to navigate her way towards Aarav.

"Avoiding the dance floor, Mr. Singhania?" she asked, her voice light and teasing as she reached him.

"No, watching you conquer the designer world single-handedly, Miss Oberoi," he countered, his voice a low rumble that sent a faint shiver down her spine, despite the crowded room.

"You were watching me?"

Aarav's eyes sparkled with a playful defiance.

"Just a casual observation of the room's architecture. You happened to be standing near a particularly interesting gargoyle."

Navya knew he was lying. She had seen him across the room, his gaze flickering in her direction, assessing, analyzing.

Suddenly, a woman in a heavily beaded gown approached them, her smile wide and overly enthusiastic.

"Navya, isn't this Aarav Singhania?"

"Yes, Sarah," Navya nodded. "This is him."

"Hello." Aarav smiled.

Sarah paused, then peered at them.

"You two look good together."

Aarav and Navya exchanged a look, both their hearts stopped beating for a moment.

"Mr. Singhania and I are just...discussing the finer points of design." Navya plastered on her most charming smile.

Aarav nodded, a hint of amusement in his eyes.

Sarah beamed.

"Well, whatever it is, it's captivating! You two should have a dance."

Both of them looked at the dance floor.

"Shall we?" he asked softly when he reached closer to her. He extended his hand toward her and could feel his heart pounding in his chest. It was as if the world around them had faded away suddenly, and it was just the two of them.

Navya hesitated briefly before placing her hand in his. A jolt of electricity coursed through him at their contact, and for the first time, he felt the weight of his past lift, if only for a moment. She gave him a tentative smile, her lips trembling slightly as the two walked toward the center of the gathering.

The music shifted, enveloping them in a gentle embrace. Aarav guided her, his eyes focused on her face, while she looked at the stage.

The next sound started and her steps faltered. He stopped walking and unconsciously stepped closer to her.

"This song..." she whispered, more to herself than to Aarav, her voice barely audible.

"What's wrong?" Aarav's brow furrowed, at the sudden change in Navya's mood.

Her chest tightened, and she fought the swell of emotions rising like a tide.

"It just... reminds me of..." she said, her voice trailing off.

"Of?"

"Of something... Something I don't want to remember," she replied after composing herself. She quickly turned to the crowded dance floor, avoiding his searching gaze.

"Miss Oberoi?" Aarav gently whispered her name, grounding her back into reality.

"I'm sorry," she breathed out. "Sometimes I just remember... how it used to feel, you know?"

Aarav softly placed a hand on her shoulder and nodded. He knew what it was to be reminded of the past in places where he didn't expect that to happen. How it suddenly felt like gravity became stronger and air became thicker and escaping from memories felt impossible.

"It's okay to remember, but you're here with me now," he said, speaking slowly, choosing his words with care. "You don't have to let the past dim what we have."

"I know. I didn't think I would ever be dancing like this," Navya murmured, her voice barely rising above the melody.

"Neither did I." He replied, a light chuckle escaping him.

Their laughter mingled with the music. As they circled each other, Aarav took a moment to look at Navya. Her eyes sparkled despite the depths of her history, and he found himself wanting to delve deeper, not out of mere curiosity, but out of a need to understand.

Suddenly, Aarav pulled her closer, feeling the warmth from her. As they moved together, their bodies synchronized, the tension in the atmosphere shifting from her pain and his curiosity to the electrifying chemistry between them.

"I know this is all new," Aarav bent closer to him, his breath warm against her ear. "But perhaps we can heal together. I would be lying if I said I was never waiting for someone who understands."

Navya's heart swelled at his words, and suddenly her past felt distant, the moments of darkness slowly giving way to light. She looked into his eyes, seeing a reflection of her own struggles, and a fleeting connection formed, fragile yet profound.

SEVEN

Twirling Hearts

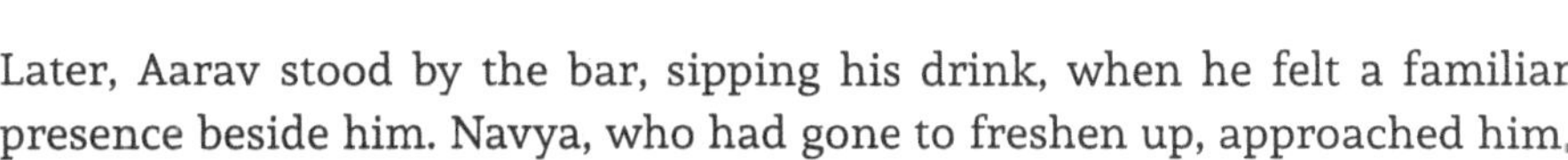

Later, Aarav stood by the bar, sipping his drink, when he felt a familiar presence beside him. Navya, who had gone to freshen up, approached him, her smile lightening up the space around her.

"Did I say, you look stunning tonight?" Aarav said, trying to sound cool, but his heart was beating fast.

Navya felt a rush of warmth spread through her as Aarav's words sank in. It was the first time he had ever complimented her, and his choice of words—stunning—was both unexpected and *overwhelming.*

She wasn't sure how to react. She tucked away a hair strand and looked down, trying to hide her crimson cheeks as she felt a mix of emotions—surprise, happiness, and a touch of nervousness.

She glanced at Aarav. He was looking at her with a sincerity that she had never seen before. His eyes seemed to soften, and for a moment, Navya felt a connection that had been missing from their earlier interactions. She wondered if this was actually the beginning of something new, a shift in their relationship that could bring them closer together.

"Thanks! You clean up pretty well yourself." She said smiling.

A wave of nervousness washed over Aarav as he processed the compliment. It was the first time they had really acknowledged each other in such a personal and positive way, and it caught him off guard in the best possible manner. When he had mustered the courage to tell her how beautiful she looked, he hadn't been sure how she would react. To hear her say that he cleans up pretty well was more than he could have hoped for.

He smiled to himself, feeling a sense of pride and a hint of bashfulness. It wasn't just about looking good; it was the validation that maybe, just maybe, they could see each other as more than just two people brought together by their families.

As they stood there, the world outside seemed to fade away. The party chatter blurred into a soft hum and for a moment, Aarav felt a sudden pull toward her. It was as if there was some magnetic connection pushing him toward her.

"Do you ever wonder where we are headed?" she asked softly, breaking the comfortable silence.

Aarav turned to her, intrigued. "In what sense?"

"In life, you know? Sometimes it feels like we're at a crossroads..." her voice trailed off, reflecting a mix of hope and uncertainty.

Aarav shifted closer, the space between them shrinking.

"I think we're already on a path. Together."

"Together?" She looked up at him.

"Yes." Aarav leaned in slightly, the tension palpable. "This arranged marriage... it feels like a compromise, but maybe... maybe it doesn't have to be."

"You are right," Navya nodded. "We both have our reasons for agreeing to this, but I don't want our lives to be defined by compromise. Not when we could make it something more."

"I want that too. I want us to be happy, Miss. Oberoi. I want us to find a way to move past our pasts and build something real together. But I want to take it slow"

"We can start small, build trust, and see where it takes us."

Navya smiled genuinely, her eyes shining with relief and hope.

"That sounds like a good plan. Let's start tonight."

"To a new beginning, Miss Oberoi," Aarav said, raising the glass.

Navya raised her glass with a smile.

"To a new beginning, Mr. Singhania."

"To us, *Navya*."

Navya's heart skipped a beat. Hearing her name spoken by him felt like a revelation, a gentle nudge towards intimacy they both had yearned for and feared. It was as if the formality fell away, revealing a new layer of their relationship.

She wanted to respond, to break the barrier she had been so cautious of, but the weight of the moment was heavy. Would it be too soon to drop the formality? Would it mean that she was ready to embrace whatever came next, or would it push them too far too fast?

She met his gaze, searching for the intention behind those words. Aarav smiled, a genuine smile that reached his eyes, and she felt her heart melt just a little more. In that moment, she realized that perhaps it was time to let go of the titles that had once provided comfort but now felt like chains. Maybe they were ready to step into a new phase together—one where they could explore the depths of who they were, not just as Mr. Singhania and Miss Oberoi, but as Aarav and Navya.

Navya clunk her glass against his.

"To us, *Aarav*."

They both take a sip, their eyes locked in a silent understanding.

The next day, Aarav and Navya stood near their model, meeting their colleagues as they waited for the announcement of the winners for the best project in the workshop.

The host, holding a clipboard, stepped up to the microphone.

"And the winner for the best project goes to... Aarav Singhania and Navya Oberoi for their innovative fusion of architecture and fashion!"

The room erupted in applause as Aarav and Navya exchanged surprised glances. They made their way to the stage.

On reaching, they exchanged a brief, knowing smile before turning to face the audience.

"We honestly didn't expect this," Aarav said gratefully. "Thank you so much to the workshop for this opportunity."

"Yes, thank you," Navya smiled. "We're truly grateful for this recognition, and we're excited to continue pushing the boundaries of our respective fields."

The Director presented them with a trophy and mementos that they humbly accepted.

"Is there more to this partnership than just a project?" asked one of the guests. "I thought I noticed some chemistry."

The murmurs grew, speculations turning to excitement. Meanwhile, Aarav and Navya shared a glance.

"You had said no one would notice," Navya whispered, making Aarav chuckle.

"Do you think they're dating? They look so good together."

They heard other guests talking as they walked down the stage. Everyone was cheering for them.

"If they aren't, they should be! Look at them."

The crowd cheered louder, the rumors escalated as they posed for photographs, the trophy gleaming between them—a symbol of their triumph, and perhaps, something more. Their smiling faces shined under the spotlight, leaving the audience spellbound.

Navya sat next to Aarav, trying to focus on the workshop proceedings, but she couldn't help feeling overwhelmed by the stares and whispers around them. She understood that people had speculated about their relationship and the rumors of their marriage. She had heard someone talk about their Instagram posts and similar captions. The constant attention and scrutiny had become too much for her to handle.

"It feels like the only thing people are talking about is us," Navya said as another group of people smiled looking at both of them. "Aarav, do you think we should just tell everyone? It might be easier."

"I don't know," Aarav said after thinking for a moment. "It's a tough call. On one hand, it might take the pressure off. On the other hand, it could turn into a media circus, and we might not get the chance to really be ourselves before the wedding."

"You're right. We need to be careful. But how do we do that without looking like we're hiding something?"

"If we act natural, people will eventually realize there's nothing to speculate about," he shrugged.

"Act natural?" Navya asked, shocked. "Is that even possible when everyone is constantly watching us? I feel like I am under surveillance all the time!"

Aarav laughed at her expression

"I guess it's a bit of a challenge, but we can do it. We're both professionals, and we can handle this," he kept his hand on hers. "And if we do decide to tell everyone, we can do it on our terms, when we are ready."

Navya nodded, though her heart started beating faster as she kept looking at Aarav's hand on hers.

EIGHT

WEDDING JITTERS

Rumors began to swirl around Aarav and Navya's impending marriage. Business associates, clients, friends, and even strangers began to whisper about their relationship. Each person added their own twist to the story. While someone claimed to have insider information, another created wild tales of secret meetings and romantic escapades.

Aarav found himself bombarded with messages from followers eager to congratulate him or inquire about the details of his relationship. Meanwhile, Navya's comments section was also filled with excitement, support, and curiosity, as people eagerly awaited confirmation of the news.

Despite the chaos, both of them remained calm. They wanted their announcement to be special and meaningful, not overshadowed by the noise of rumors.

The sun was shining brightly outside, and inside Aarav's home, there was a vibrant energy in the air. The house was decorated lavishly, and the scent of lavender filled the room. Sitting on the sofa, Aarav nervously fidgeted with his phone. It was finally happening. The first ritual of the wedding was about to start. But instead of excitement, there was a nagging sense of uneasiness. What if he was not enough for her?

He hadn't failed to note how Navya wasn't over her past relationship. The way she broke down whenever she talked about it- he could feel her pain. He wanted to be the person who helped her heal, the one who would make her feel loved and cherished. But could he really do that?

He couldn't find the courage to tell Samaira how he felt, and here he was, about to enter into a marriage where feelings were supposed to be mutual. He felt like he was a living paradox, a man who had failed to express his emotions now stepping into a lifelong commitment.

His family members were bustling around, setting up for the ceremony and giggling as they passed by Aarav.

"Are you excited or just looking at the Mehendi designs?" Megha asked, sitting beside him.

Aarav rolled his eyes.

"I am just... mentally preparing for all the events."

"Then prepare yourself well for the sangeet and just try not to trip over your feet when Navya Bhabhi walks in," Sahil said grinning.

Megha burst into laughter, and Aarav couldn't help but chuckle as well, shaking his head in disbelief.

"I won't trip over! I'm a great dancer, thank you very much. It's just... this is a big day, you know?"

Megha looked at him and could see the nervous energy radiating off him. She knew this moment was significant for him, a blend of excitement and apprehension that came with the territory of an arranged marriage. Her protective sisterly instincts rose as she held his hand.

Aarav had always been reserved. She remembered the countless times she had confided in him and had shared her dreams, fears, and the pressures of family expectations. Now, it was her turn to be there for him, to help him navigate.

"Aarav," she began gently, her voice steady but warm. "I know you're feeling overwhelmed right now. It's completely normal to be nervous about this. It's a big step, and it's okay to have mixed emotions."

She watched as he took a deep breath, the tension in his shoulders easing slightly.

"Remember, this isn't just about the functions. It's about building a life together. You have the opportunity to get to know her, to create something special."

Aarav glanced up at her, his expression a mix of uncertainty and hope.

"What if I fail to be a good husband?" he asked, vulnerability spilling from his words. "What if I disappoint her?"

Megha leaned forward, her eyes locking onto his.

"You won't disappoint her just by being yourself. And if you have problems sometimes, that's okay too. Relationships take time to grow. Just keep an open heart and mind. You both have the chance to discover each other."

As she spoke, Megha could feel the weight of his worries beginning to lift. She wanted him to know that love could blossom in the most unexpected ways, even in an arranged marriage.

"Think of it as a journey. You'll learn and grow together, and who knows? You might find that you have more in common than you think."

Aarav nodded slowly, a flicker of hope igniting in his eyes. Megha smiled, feeling a sense of relief washed over her. She reached out and squeezed his hand, grounding him in the moment.

As Navya sat with her knees bent to allow the Mehndi artist access to her feet, the rich scent of henna filled the air, swirling around her like a comforting embrace.

She looked at her parents. They were smiling, their faces radiant with joy, yet she couldn't help but feel conflicted. It was hard to reconcile their happiness with the uncertainty that lingers in her mind. Would she fit into Aarav's family?

Her trust was shattered and her heart still stung at the memory of her broken dreams. Sometimes she wondered if she was actually ready to open her heart again. Aarav was a good man, and she knew he cared about her, but what if she was not able to give him what he deserved? She had seen the pain love could cause, and it terrified her.

But then she thought of Aarav - his quiet strength and the kindness in his eyes. He had been patient and supportive, always respecting her boundaries. She felt a flicker of hope that maybe, just maybe, this could be different. Perhaps they could create something beautiful together, despite their pasts.

Yet, the jitters lingered, and she wondered if she would ever be able to shake off the fear of getting hurt again.

"The design is so beautiful, beta," her mother Anjali said, her voice a little too bright. She reached out to gently touch Navya's hand, careful not to smudge the wet henna. "It's like they're painting a whole new future onto your palms."

Navya forced a smile.

"It is lovely, Mom," but the words felt brittle, like dried leaves crumbling in her mouth.

"Remember, Navya," Anjali continued, her voice softening, almost a whisper, "a family is built on compromise. Don't be afraid to speak your mind, but also be willing to bend like the willow. We all have our ways, and they might be different from what you're used to."

Navya understood the unspoken fear in her mother's words. A past that her family had tried to bury, a past filled with harsh words and a suffocating silence. Her mother knew she had had a painful lesson that had left her with a deep-rooted insecurity about her worthiness of love.

"I know, Mom," Navya murmured, her voice barely audible. "But what if... what if I can't?" The question, raw and vulnerable, escaped before she could reign it in.

Her mother instantly understood. The forced cheerfulness dropped away, replaced by a familiar tenderness. She knelt beside Navya, taking her other hand, her touch a grounding force.

“You can, Navya. You will,” she said, her voice firm now, full of a mother's unwavering belief. "You are strong, my daughter. Stronger than you give yourself credit for. This is different. Their family is different."

She paused, choosing her words carefully.

“It's just Aarav and his siblings. But branches of the same tree grow in different directions. Don't let that worry you. What matters is the heart at the center. And from what I have seen, Aarav has a good one. And so do you. You deserve happiness, Navya, don't ever forget that.”

The henna artist paused, wiping her brow. “Almost done,” she announced, a smile playing on her lips.

Navya glanced down at her hands, watching as the artist meticulously worked on her mehendi. The swirls and curves began to take shape, much like the journey she was about to embark on. Each stroke felt like a promise- a promise of understanding, of new beginnings.

NINE
THE D-DAY

Aarav bolted upright in bed, his heart hammering against his ribs. The cotton sheets clung to him, damp with a cold sweat that had nothing to do with the bedroom temperature. He took a shaky breath, his eyes wide, trying to piece together the fragments of the nightmare that still clung to the edges of his mind.

He had the nightmare again. A car accident, *visceral and terrifying.* He had been in the car, and he had seen it all with excruciating clarity. The screech of tires on asphalt, the sickening crunch of metal on metal, the shattering of glass like a crystalline scream.

Another vehicle moving in the wrong direction, moving too fast, going around the curve, and had lost control, spinning before slamming onto the car. The image was seared into his memory, a memory so strong that he couldn't shake it.

Aarav ran a hand through his hair, the strands sticking to his forehead. He knew, with a certainty that chilled him to the bone. It had been six years already, but he still had those nightmares.

He looked towards the clock, it was time to wake up, he had a meeting in an hour.

The air buzzed with a vibrant energy, thick with the scent of marigolds and the melody of a Bollywood remix. The Sangeet ceremony for Aarav and Navya was in full swing, transforming the sprawling lawn of Navya's family home into a kaleidoscope of colors and laughter. Fairy lights draped across the trees winked like scattered stars, casting a warm glow on the swirling figures below.

The Sangeet. The night when two families come together and when laughter and music are supposed to drown out everything. The loud music was a cacophony and the dance performances a blur for Navya. She forced a smile, a practiced smile that didn't quite reach her eyes. Everyone kept saying she looked beautiful. But inside that elaborate garb, she felt distressed.

It was meant to be *him.* She had her life mapped out, a future painted in shades of laughter and shared dreams. But fate, that cruel artist, had decided to splatter a black canvas over her masterpiece. Now, here she was, on the precipice of a new life with Aarav.

She saw Aarav sitting beside her. He was watching his cousins perform a dance number with a detached expression. He looked lost, like he was watching a play he was not quite a part of. The months leading up to the wedding had been a whirlwind of meetings, ceremonies, and frantic arrangements. Balancing work, families, and the sheer mountain of tasks required to plan an Indian wedding had left them little time for anything else, let alone dance rehearsals. Both had optimistically planned to attend a few classes, "next week," but "next week" had never quite arrived. The result? A spectacular sangeet, without the bride and the groom performing.

Navya cleared her throat to gain Aarav's attention. Aarav turned, his dark eyes meeting hers. For a brief moment, she saw a flicker of something there – was it sadness? Or just weariness?

"You like dancing?" she asked, her voice barely audible above the music.

"Not a hobby, but I dance pretty well," he said smiling.

"Mind showing me some moves?"

"Why, you want me to dance for you?"

Just then, Megha approached them, her face beaming.

"Enough of your couple talks! Now it's time to steal the show. Move!"

Navya and Aarav exchanged a look of sheer terror.

"Actually, Megha," Navya began, her voice wavering slightly, "we haven't...uh...we haven't really had time to... rehearse."

"Nonsense!" she said with a wave of her hand. "It's just a dance, the important thing is to have fun! Come on, you two, the music is calling!" She grabbed both their hands and practically dragged them towards the dance floor.

As they were thrust into the spotlight, the music changed to a romantic, almost melancholic tune, a classic Bollywood number that everyone knew. Navya's heart thumped against her ribs. She could feel the weight of a hundred pairs of eyes on them, waiting, anticipating.

"Relax, we have danced together before," Aarav whispered as he took her hand, his grip firm.

"But no one looked at us like this then," Navya said but one look into his eyes, and she forgot her anxiety.

And then, Aarav began to sway gently to the rhythm of the music, his movements awkward but endearing. Navya followed suit, her body responding to the familiar melody.

They stumbled, they almost collided, but through it all, they maintained a connection. They locked eyes, a silent communication passing between them, a mutual understanding that this was okay, even beautiful in its imperfection.

The crowd, initially expectant, now seemed to be caught up in the raw emotion of the moment. They clapped and cheered, their faces beaming with genuine warmth. They weren't applauding a polished performance; they were celebrating Navya and Aarav, just as they were.

As the song faded, Navya realized that the lack of rehearsal, the initial anxiety, it had all been a blessing in disguise. In their uncoordinated dance, they had discovered a new kind of connection, a shared laugh in the midst of chaos. They may not have had a rehearsed dance, but they had shared a truly authentic moment. And that, Navya knew, was more beautiful than any choreographed performance could ever be. The sangeet, despite its initial hiccup, was turning out to be perfect, in its own wonderfully messy way.

Later, Aarav found himself standing beside Navya, both slightly breathless from the dancing. He noticed the delicate henna patterns on her hands, intricate and beautiful.

"You were amazing," Navya said.

"So were you," he replied, teasingly. "For someone who doesn't dance."

She chuckled, a low, rumbling sound that surprised both of them.

"I never said I don't dance."

Aarav looked at her with a frown and Navya burst out laughing. Aarav smiled seeing her laugh.

As her laughter dried down, they stood in comfortable silence for a moment, watching the festivities unfold around them. The air was filled with the sweet aroma of jasmine and the rhythmic beat of the dhol. It was a vibrant, chaotic scene, yet in that moment, they found a quiet intimacy.

The Sangeet was more than just music and dance; it was a bridge, a celebration of new beginnings. And, as the night wore on, with the music still playing and the laughter still echoing, both Aarav and Navya knew that this was just the beginning of their story. *The story they were yet to write.*

On the day of the wedding, Navya stared at her reflection, the ornate lehenga feeling like a shimmering cage. It was designed by herself, it was beautiful, undeniably so, but the weight of it mirrored the weight in her chest. She traced the intricate embroidery, her fingers lingering on the delicate threads. This was supposed to be the happiest day, the start of something new, but *a tremor of fear ran under the surface of her excitement.* Memories, like shards of glass, flickered at the edges of her mind. The ghost of a past relationship, the hurt, the betrayal – they tried to wedge themselves into her present joy.

She took a deep breath. This wasn't then. This was now, with Aarav. A gentle warmth spread through her at his name. He wasn't like the others. He was patient and understanding, his quiet strength was a balm to her anxieties. But still, the question lingered: could she truly let go of the past and embrace this future she was building? The pressure to be perfect, to be the happy bride, felt immense. A small, almost imperceptible smile touched her lips. She would try. *She would be brave.* She deserved this happiness, and she would be happy.

♡♡♡

TEN

Veiled in Vermilion, Blinded by Vengeance

Aarav, usually so composed in his tailored suits for work, felt a bead of sweat trickle down his temple despite the cool air conditioning. He sat on the ornately decorated mandap, his brocade sherwani feeling suddenly heavy, the weight mirroring the weight of the moment. Beside him, veiled in red and gold, sat Navya. He could only see the delicate curve of her cheek, the glint of her jewelry, but he could feel her presence as strongly as the beat of his own heart.

The pandit chanted in a rhythmic Sanskrit, his voice resonating with ancient blessings. The *gathbandhan* was next. Aarav watched, captivated, as Avni carefully tied a silken scarf, laden with auspicious symbols, to the end of his shawl and Navya's dupatta. The knot felt significant, a tangible representation of the bond they were about to forge, not just between themselves, but also between their families. He glanced at Navya's parents, their faces etched with pride and hope. He knew they believed in this, in the power of tradition, in the promise of a future built on shared values.

"You look like you've seen a ghost!" Megha whispered in his ears, earning a glare from him. "Relax! She's not going to run away...unless you give her a good reason to!"

The teasing, usually comforting, felt amplified under the pressure of the moment. Aarav forced a laugh, trying to ignore the knot tightening in his stomach. He caught his siblings eyes, their faces a mask of serene joy.

Then came the *sindoor*. The priest chanted mantras and Aarav felt his heart hammer against his ribs. This was it. The defining moment. The act that would publicly declare them husband and wife. He took a deep breath, trying to steady his trembling hand.

He reached for the small silver box containing the vermillion powder. Navya lowered her veil slightly, her dark eyes lined with kohl, meeting his for the briefest of seconds. He saw a flicker of... nervousness? Excitement? Hope? He couldn't quite decipher it, but it mirrored the tumultuous emotions churning within him.

He dipped his finger into the silver box, the vibrant red a stark contrast against his skin. With reverence, he carefully applied it to the parting of her hair. He felt a strange mix of humility and power – the power to begin a new life, the humility to understand the responsibility that came with it.

He stepped back slightly, his gaze locked on the crimson streak that now adorned her forehead. Navya looked ethereal, transformed. The sindoor seemed to illuminate her face, highlighting her delicate features, making her even more beautiful.

"*Dulha and Dulhan* may now stand up for the phera's."

As they walked around the sacred fire, each step symbolizing a promise, Aarav found himself focusing on Navya. He noticed the intricate embroidery on her lehenga, the delicate jingle of her anklets, the way her hand trembled slightly as she held his. He was acutely aware of her presence beside him, a woman he barely knew, yet someone he was about to pledge his life to.

As the wedding rituals completed, Aarav and Navya stood beside each other with smiles on their faces.

Megha, Aryan and Avni practically bounced with joy.

"See, I told you they were perfect together! They look like they stepped right out of a fairytale!" Avni exclaimed, clasping her hands together.

Aryan nodded enthusiastically.

"Yeah, even I have to admit, they're a perfect match."

"You all need to thank someone here," Megha said, pretending to wave at everyone, proud of herself.

"Congratulations, Jijaji," Kavya, with her ever enthusiastic voice rushed towards them. "You've survived the gauntlet."

Aarav chuckled, while Navya looked at her sister amused.

"Thanks, Kavya. It's... a lot to take in."

"Tell me about it," she grinned, a mischievous glint in her eyes. "I have seen this happen a few times, and it never gets any less overwhelming. Just remember to breathe."

"Sage advice," Aarav said, smiling. "Thank you."

All of them burst out laughing.

"My sister is incredibly intelligent and kind, though. And fiercely loyal. You'll see," Kavya paused, then added with a playful nudge, "Just... try not to bore her, okay? She has a low tolerance for dull conversations."

Aarav laughed again, finding himself surprisingly at ease with Navya's sister. "Duly noted. I'll try to keep things interesting."

"Good," Kavya said, her smile genuine. "Welcome to the family, Jiju. I have a feeling we're going to have a lot of fun!"

Then Megha, Kavya, Aryan and Avni went towards the other cousins who were looking like they were definitely having some fun.

Aarav looked at Navya, who was already looking at him. He still felt a wave of apprehension, but mixed with it was a flicker of anticipation. Maybe, just maybe, this arranged marriage wouldn't be so bad after all. He had a feeling Kavya was right. They were going to have a lot of fun. And perhaps, in time, he and Navya would build something truly special, bound not just by tradition, but by affection and understanding.

A buzz on his phone broke Aarav's trance.

Mishra calling - it read.

"Hello?" He picked up the phone.

"It's Rajesh Oberoi's daughter."

Aarav stood frozen, phone pressed to his ear, the voice on the other end a steady, professional drone, yet each word a hammer blew against the fragile walls of his happiness. His breath hitched in his chest, refusing to cooperate, each inhale a shallow, painful rasp.

He looked at Navya, a radiant smile on her face.

"Are you absolutely certain?" Aarav managed to croak, his voice a strained whisper, barely recognizable even to himself.

"Positive, Mr. Singhania. Cross-referenced, verified through multiple sources. There's no room for error."

Aarav's world tilted, the wedding hall blurring at the edges.

He closed his eyes, a dizzying swirl of emotions crashing through him. Disbelief warred with a cold, insidious dread that was already creeping through his veins, turning his blood to ice. He looked at Navya again, her eyes sparkled with anticipation for their future, their future... a future that now felt like a colossal, cruel joke.

He vaguely heard the person on the phone continuing, laying out the details, the evidence, each sentence like a shard of glass piercing his soul. But the words began to lose their meaning, dissolving into a muffled hum in his ears. His mind was a chaotic storm, whipped by confusion, betrayal, and a rising sense of something akin to horror.

How could this be? The woman he knew, the woman he thought he knew, the woman he is now married to, the woman he just pledged his life to... was she really capable of... this?

The information was a viper coiled in his heart. How could Navya do this? He would confront her. He would make sure she pays for what she has done. He envisioned the public humiliation, the dramatic reveal, the shocked gasps of the guests. He could almost taste the sweet vindication, the righteous anger that would sear through the facade of their perfect arranged marriage. But the image was fragmented, broken by the sight of two faces: *Aryan's and Avni's.*

They walked towards them, their eyes full of emotions.

"I... I just want to say that, I am glad you are a part of our family." Aryan said, his voice unusually vulnerable. "It's just... you get us, you know?"

Aarav rarely saw that side of his fiercely independent brother.

"Yeah! Like, Mom... Mom was great, but you... you actually listen." Avni added. "You understand us."

"Hey, you two," Navya held both of them closer. "I know I can never replace her, but I promise I'll make sure you miss her less."

That lit up Avni's face, and Aryan's shoulders seemed to relax.

Aarav's breath caught on his throat. For five years he was trying to fill that impossible void. And Navya, somehow, had managed to ease the pain.

He had seen Aryan, his usually carefree brother, actually seeming grounded for once. Navya had a knack for understanding Aryan's sometimes erratic energy, guiding him with a gentle patience.

And Avni... his sweet, shy little sister. She had blossomed under Navya's gentle encouragement. Before Navya, Avni had retreated into herself, a ghost haunting the edges of their lives since their parents passed away five years ago. Now, she was laughing, participating in life, her eyes sparkling with newfound confidence.

"I... I don't even miss her as much now," Avni confessed, her voice thick with emotion. "Not since you, *Bhabhi.*"

Aarav felt a physical blow to his chest. He couldn't do it. He couldn't snatch away that fragile solace he had seen bloom in his siblings' faces. He couldn't risk sending Avni back into her silent shell, or watch Aryan retreat into his studied indifference. They needed her. They needed Navya.

But their unadulterated happiness twisted something inside Aarav, a mixture of guilt and a cold, bitter resolve.

He wanted to tell them to yank the veil of illusion from their eyes. He had wanted to expose Navya for who she truly was, to shout the secret that had burned a hole of molten rage in his soul. But he didn't. He saw her smiling at his siblings. *That smile.* He would snatch it away. He wouldn't let Navya live in peace. He would stay married to her, yes, but he would make sure she understood the price she would pay for this unexpected victory. *He would make her life a living hell.*

He pulled Navya closer, a possessive gesture that elicited a soft gasp from her.

"Get ready for a roller coaster journey, *Mrs. Singhania,*" he whispered, his voice so low only she could hear it. The endearment was a weapon, the 'Mrs. Singhania' dripping with sarcasm she seemed oblivious to.

Her smile widened.

For the first time, Aarav saw not the woman his siblings adored, but a person capable of the most profound deceit. He saw the future, a bleak landscape where his every action would be measured, every word a calculated move. He would be the master of her cage, and she would be the pampered prisoner, completely oblivious to the bars that surrounded her.

"Thank you for everything, Aarav." She said with a hint of happy tears in her eyes.

"This is just the beginning."

Aarav took her hand in his, interlocking their fingers. It was a promise, a dark vow made in the heart of the night, a pledge that her life would never be the same again. As he stared at her, he knew that the secret he held was a weapon, a key to control.

The real show was about to begin.

TURNING TIDES

ELEVEN

SHATTERED DREAMS

Navya sat on the edge of the bed, her heart beating fast with a mix of excitement and nervousness. The room was beautifully decorated, a reflection of the care and attention her new family had put into making her feel welcome. She had spent the past few months preparing for this moment, imagining what it would be like to start a new life with Aarav.

She glanced at the ornate mirror, her reflection a strange mix of unfamiliar finery and quiet apprehension. The kohl outlined her eyes, making them appear larger. She barely recognised the woman staring back, a woman adorned in hues of red and gold, a woman who was now a *wife.*

A wave of nervousness washed over her, leaving her stomach in a knot. What would her life be like? Would they have things to talk about? She had hoped that this journey would be beautiful, where they could build a life together, filled with if not love, but respect.

As she waited for Aarav to join her, Navya's thoughts drifted to her family. Her parents and sister had been overjoyed at the match. Her sister, Kavya had seen her in her worst state, so she was definitely the happiest. Navya felt a deep sense of gratitude for their support, but also a twinge of uncertainty about what lay ahead. She had always been independent and strong-willed, and she wondered how those traits would fit into her new role as a wife.

Aarav finally entered the room, and Navya's heart skipped a beat. But as she looked into his eyes, she saw a storm of emotions that she couldn't quite place. There was anger, but also something else—pain, perhaps, or frustration. She felt a sudden urge to reach out to him, to understand what was troubling him, but before she could, he spoke.

"Don't," he said, his voice laced with venom. "Just ... don't."

Navya's brow furrowed. This wasn't the welcome she'd expected. She swallowed, trying to quell her rising panic.

"Aarav, is something wrong?"

Without another word, Aarav moved with a deliberate stiffness, like a puppet controlled by unseen strings. He tossed his wedding turban onto a nearby chair and began to walk towards the balcony.

"Aarav," she held his arm, making him face her. "What happened?"

Aarav moved closer, his presence suddenly overwhelming, filling the small space between them. He leaned in, his voice dropped to a menacing whisper.

"Let me make one thing perfectly clear. Don't ever try to assert your right to be my wife," he took her hands of his arm.

But his words cut through Navya like shards of ice. She felt a tear escape, tracing a lonely path down her cheek. Her voice trembled as she spoke.

"But... but why? What did I do?"

"You *exist*. That's your crime. And now you're here, in my house, in my life. And believe me, Navya, I will make your life a living hell. You are now at my mercy and there is no escape for you." Aarav said, his voice cold and devoid of any emotion.

Navya felt the room spin. Her heart, which had been fluttering with anticipation, now plummeted to her stomach. She stared at Aarav, her eyes wide with shock and confusion.

"What do you mean?" she managed to ask, her voice trembling.

Aarav's expression remained unchanged.

"Exactly what I said," he replied, his tone flat. "You don't even realise what you have gotten into after marrying me. Now, I am going to make sure you regret it every single day."

Navya's mind raced, trying to make sense of what she had just heard. This couldn't be happening. It was a dream, a nightmare. She shook her head, as if trying to wake up from the dream.

"No, Aarav, you don't mean it. You are joking, right?"

But Aarav's eyes told a different story. They were cold, unfeeling.

"I meant every word," he said, his voice barely a whisper. "I am not a funny person Navya, I don't joke around you know that."

Navya's initial shock began to give way to a desperate need to deny what was happening.

"No, no, no," she repeated, her voice rising in pitch. "This isn't real. We can fix this. Just tell me what went wrong, I..."

"I don't have time for your melodrama," Aarav turned away and left the room, the door closing behind him with a finality that echoed in her ears. Navya's denial began to waver.

She felt a surge of anger rising within her, a fiery emotion that burned through her veins. How could he say such things? How could he treat her this way? She had done nothing to deserve this.

Tears of rage and hurt streamed down her face as she sat on the edge of the bed, her fists clenched. She wanted to scream, to lash out, to throw a tantrum but the walls of the room seemed to close in around her, suffocating her. She was trapped, not just in this room, but in a marriage that had turned into a living nightmare.

As the night wore on, Navya's anger began to mix with a desperate urge to find a way out. She started to bargain with herself, with the universe, with anyone who might be listening.

"If I just try harder, if I can just sort it out, maybe there is some misunderstanding," she thought. "Maybe he just needs time to adjust. We can make this work."

But the more she thought about it, the more she realized the futility of her bargaining. Aarav's words had been clear, and the coldness in his eyes had been unmistakable. She was beginning to accept that this was not a misunderstanding or a momentary lapse. This was the beginning of a new reality.

The weight of this acceptance was heavy, and it brought with it a deep sense of depression. Navya lay on the bed, her body feeling like lead, her spirit crushed. The future she had envisioned, the life she had dreamed of, now seemed like a distant, unattainable dream once again.

Aarav clenched his hands into fists as he stood by on the terrace, under the bright stars. His room was filled with the scent of fresh flowers, an attempt to make the atmosphere feel more inviting, but to him, it only added to the suffocating tension. His heart pounded with a mix of frustration and helplessness. He couldn't even stand in a room where Navya was.

The news, just after the wedding, had hit him like a bolt of lightning. It had shattered the fragile hopes and expectations Aarav had had from the marriage.

He couldn't help but feel that fate had played a cruel joke on him, by even bringing him face to face with Navya, let alone marrying her. But now, he was determined to have his revenge and for Navya to have her punishment. He vowed that he would not let Navya live in peace. The idea of making her life hell seemed like the only way to find some semblance of justice.

As the first rays of sunlight began to peek through the curtains, Navya looked around, she was on the bed - Aarav's bed, *alone*. She didn't come back to the room. Flashes of last night started forming in her head again. How she was waiting for him, how she was excited for this new beginning and how he had rejected her.

Navya knew she had to face the day and the reality that lay ahead. She had to find a way to navigate this new, terrifying world. She took a deep breath, trying to anchor herself in the present. She was strong, and she would find a way to survive. But the path ahead was unclear, and the journey would be long and painful.

Her acceptance was not a surrender. It was a recognition of the challenge she now faced. She would not give up, but she knew that the road to healing and finding a way forward would be fraught with obstacles. For now, she would take one step at a time, hoping that somewhere along the way, she would find the strength to rebuild her life.

A buzz from her phone broke her trance. The notification blinked insistently, and she tapped it open, expecting it to be one of her friends or perhaps a client. Instead, her heart skipped a beat as she saw the familiar logo of Instagram.

She swiped to open the post, her eyes widening as the screen filled with a high-resolution, professionally edited image of her and Aarav standing side by side on their wedding day, their hands clasped together. The caption read:

"In love and in business. #ForeverTogether #DreamTeam."

Her breath caught in her throat as she realized what she was seeing - a public declaration of their marriage, something they had both agreed to keep private until they both felt ready to share it with the world.

Navya's mind raced. Last night, he had told point-blank that he didn't want her to assert any rights as his wife. The words stung, and she couldn't help but feel like she was being pushed away, like her emotions and their relationship didn't matter to him. How could he say one thing and do another? The blatant hypocrisy of it all was a slap in the face. Her blood ran cold and then hot with a furious energy. How could he? How could he so casually tell her one thing with his words and then completely contradict it with his actions? Did he change his mind overnight, or was this just a facade to keep up appearances?

It wasn't just about the public announcement; it was about the complete lack of respect. Keeping it private had been their joint decision, so announcing it should have been a mutual decision as well. He hadn't even bothered to give her a heads-up. Was she supposed to just play along, act like nothing was wrong? Was she expected to be the happy, supportive wife while he treated her like a stranger in private? The hollowness in her chest intensified. This wasn't a marriage; it was a performance, a spectacle designed for an audience. And she was the unwilling actress, forced to play a role she hadn't signed up for. She felt like an idiot for ever believing there was even a possibility of understanding between them.

No, he could not dictate her and her life like this. She was not someone who would tolerate all the tantrums of a man just because he was her husband. She was independent, successful. She would now pay him back in the same coin, *with interest.*

TWELVE

The Battle of Egos

Navya adjusted her earring as stood before the mirror. She wore a *salwaar kameez,* her hair, usually left unbound and playful, was now neatly parted, a thin line of *sindoor* a bold crimson against her hairline. It felt strange, this vibrant declaration of her married status. The *mangalsutra,* a delicate string of black and gold beads, rested warm and weighty against her collarbone, a constant reminder of the sacred vows she had exchanged just yesterday. She took a deep breath, a nervous tremor running through her. She couldn't bring herself to not wear the symbols of their marriage, even after Aarav's declaration last night.

As she stepped out of the room, the aroma of freshly brewed cardamom tea wafted through the air. She could hear soft murmurs and the clinking of cutlery from the dining room. Gathering her courage, she walked towards the sound, her footsteps a little hesitant.

"Bhabhi! Good morning! You look... wow!" Aryan grinned, his dimples deepening. He stopped just short of teasing her, his respect for her position as the new bride evident in his tone.

Beside him stood Avni, her face lit up with genuine warmth. She rushed forward, engulfing Navya in a light hug.

"Bhabhi, you look absolutely stunning! That color really suits you," she said, her eyes twinkling. "We were waiting for you to come down. We've got so much planned for your first day!"

Navya's nervous tension eased a bit. A small smile touched her lips, her apprehension replaced with a flicker of warmth. She felt a sense of welcome radiate from both Aryan and Avni, a comforting reassurance, which of course, Aarav had failed to provide her.

"Good morning to you too," she responded, with a smile. "Thank you both."

"You are welcome!"

Avni took Navya's hand, guiding her towards the table.

"Yes, and we have a surprise for you too! Later, of course," she added with a conspiratorial wink.

"Ah... Avni, where is your Bhai?" Navya asked as they were half way through their breakfast, and Aarav hadn't joined them.

Avni looked up at her as she munched on her sandwich.

"He went to the office early today, Kanta didi said he didn't even have breakfast."

Navya looked at Kanta, the cook who nodded. After making sure Aryan went to college and Avni to the school on time, Navya rushed to Aarav's office. The building was modern and sleek, *a testament to Aarav's talent and ambition*. As she stepped out of the elevator, she saw him sitting at his desk, scrolling through his phone with a satisfied smile on his face.

Aarav leaned back in his chair, sipping his whiskey, the bitter liquid mirroring the emotions he harbored. *This was another step towards Navya's destruction.* To make sure she wouldn't be able to escape the marriage even if she was thinking of doing so. He was determined to break her spirit, to make her question everything she had ever believed.

"Aarav!" he heard Navya call out, her voice sharp and demanding.

Aarav looked up, his smile faltering as he saw the anger in her eyes.

"What are you doing here?"

"Don't play dumb with me!" she snapped, slamming her phone down on his desk. "Why did you post that on Instagram?"

"What's the big deal? It's just a post."

Navya's anger boiled over.

"Just a post? You know very well that I had all the right to be a part of this decision if it was happening! What are you trying to achieve by doing this?"

Aarav leaned back in his chair, his eyes cold and calculating.

"I am trying to achieve a lot, actually. My business is about to launch a major project, and this kind of publicity will be beneficial. People will see us as a perfect, successful couple, and it will attract more clients."

Navya was stunned. Her confusion only deepened as she tried to reconcile the public image Aarav had crafted with the private reality he had revealed the past night. Had he been playing a role for the benefit of his business, while she had been left in the dark, hurt and betrayed? She wondered how long this had been going on, how many other times he had pretended to be something he wasn't.

She had trusted Aarav, believed in their relationship, and now she felt like a prop in his online showcase. Her heart ached with a mix of disappointment and anger. How could he do this to her? She thought they had a connection, something real, but it seemed that for Aarav, their relationship was just another tool to advance his career.

"You hired a PR firm to manage this? This is about your business, not about us?"

Aarav's lips curled into a smug smile.

"I already have a PR team. The one that manages my social media, remember? And you should be grateful, Navya. This could help your fashion label too, you know."

Navya felt a mix of betrayal and confusion.

"Grateful? Grateful for what? For hurting me? For trapping me in all this crap? You can't dictate my life Aarav, I am going back to my house!"

Aarav's smile faded, and his eyes hardened.

"Don't even think of it," he said, coming closer. "You are not going to do that, we can never be successful as a couple, but don't make me do something I don't want to do. You have worked so hard to reach where you are today, Navya. And you don't want to ruin all that you have made, do you?"

Navya's breath caught in her throat.

"What do you mean by that? You will sabotage my career?"

Aarav stood up, his posture was tense but expression was unreadable.

"I am doing what's best for my business. And if that means using our marriage to get ahead, so be it."

Navya felt a surge of determination.

"Well, you can't control everything, Aarav. I won't stand for this. I am going to take steps to protect my reputation and my business."

Aarav's eyes flickered with a hint of surprise, but he quickly masked it with a dismissive wave.

"Go ahead, Navya. I am anything but afraid of you. This is just the beginning. You'll see."

Navya turned on her heel, her mind racing with the implications of Aarav's actions.

"I hate you, Aarav Singhania," she said, walking towards the elevator.

"Oh, the feelings are mutual, wife!" He said with a smirk as he watched her leave. "Hey, Navya. Don't be late while grooming yourself for the reception party tonight!"

Navya stomped her foot as she stormed out of his office, she knew that this was not just a battle of egos; it was a fight for her future, her career and her marriage.

THIRTEEN
Perfect Couple

Navya's hands trembled slightly as she adjusted the delicate lace of her designer gown. Tears welled in her eyes, but she blinked them away, determined to maintain a facade of perfection. The change in Aarav had been sudden and sharp, like a blade cutting through the fabric of their new life together.

Yet, as she prepared for their first public appearance as a married couple, Navya felt a complex mix of emotions. Part of her considered the option of simply not showing up, of fleeing from the charade that their marriage had become. But as she looked at herself, the reflection revealed not just a woman in a beautiful dress, but a woman with a reputation to uphold, a family to honor, and a life she had built that she wasn't ready to abandon.

She couldn't bear the thought of disappointing her parents. They had so much faith in her and in the future, she was supposed to have with Aarav. She knew they would not be able to accept that they might have made a wrong decision for their daughter. Aarav wore a mask very cunningly, but to walk away now would be to admit defeat, to let Aarav's cruelty decide her and her choices.

Moreover, she was a fashion designer and a creator of beauty and elegance. She had built her career on the strength of her creativity and her ability to present the best version of herself to the world.

She took a slow breath to calm the roiling in her stomach, walking towards the grand hall.

Aarav, standing a few feet away, was the epitome of a dashing groom. His tailored sherwani fit him perfectly, his smile – the one he reserved for the audience, not her – was dazzling. He was surrounded by their families, all eager to congratulate the happy couple. Navya could feel his indifference like a cold draft, even from this distance. She was just a prop in his perfect picture, nothing more.

She put on a soft smile, one that would grace an otherwise happily married newly wedded woman's lips. Aarav wanted to maintain the illusion of a perfect marriage in front of the families from both sides. Navya too, couldn't afford to let anyone see the cracks, not when so much was at stake. Her career, her family's reputation, and her new family's happiness, everything depended on it.

Steeling herself, she lifted her chin higher, plastered a smile on her face, and began to walk. It was a slow, measured walk, her gaze sweeping across the room, making eye contact with those who looked her way.

She spotted her friends from college, a cluster of brightly dressed women, their faces alight with nervous excitement. Instead of shrinking away – as she had been doing all day – she veered towards them.

"Hey guys!" she greeted them, her voice ringing with a confidence that surprised even her. "It's so wonderful to see you. I am so glad you could make it."

The girls practically gushed, their relief palpable. They had been worried for her, she could see it in their eyes. They knew what she had gone through in her past relationship.

"Nav, we are so glad you are happy!" said Gia, one of her friends.

Navya laughed, a genuine sound, and engaged them in lively conversation, asking about their lives, making jokes, her wit sharper than they had ever seen. She wasn't falling apart, she wasn't wilting under the weight of her supposed misfortune. She was shining.

Aarav, sensing a shift in the atmosphere, excused himself from his friends and approached.

"Navya," he started, his voice smooth and low, "I was wondering where you had gone," he placed his hand lightly at the small of her back, a gesture meant to convey intimacy to the onlookers.

She turned to him, her smile as radiant as ever.

"Just catching up with some friends," she slipped her own hand over his, her touch light, almost fleeting. "It's important to have strong friendships, don't you think?"

His eyes narrowed slightly, a flicker of surprise in their depths. *She was playing along.*

"Of course," he replied, recovering quickly. He tightened his grip on her hand slightly, his smile unwavering. "They're lovely. Perhaps we should all mingle together?"

Navya's smile did not falter, but a flash of defiance danced in her eyes.

"Absolutely," she agreed, her voice laced with a sweet, silken tone that didn't quite reach her heart. "It would be wonderful to introduce my friends to my husband."

She knew that every eye in the room was on them. They were a picture-perfect couple, the epitome of marital bliss. But Navya knew the truth. She knew that beneath the surface, a battle was brewing. She was no longer a helpless wife. She was a warrior in disguise, and the reception was her first battlefield. She intended to win.

The PR team had briefed them on how to maintain the facade of a perfect couple. Navya found it increasingly difficult to keep up the act but Aarav was effortlessly acting as if this was the best day of his life.

He greeted each guest with a handshake, his charming smile never wavering. Navya watched him from the corner of her eye, her heart aching with each false laugh and polite nod he offered.

"I knew there was something brewing," said Manav, Aarav's friend. "It all started at the seminar, isn't it?"

Aarav laughed.

"It was much before that. I didn't want anyone to know what a charming woman I had before she was all mine."

Navya knew he was acting, but him being so effortlessly warm to everyone else while treating her with such coldness was almost unbearable. He spoke to everyone with ease, his words flowing smoothly, and Navya could see why people were so taken by him.

As the night wore on, Navya found a few moments of respite. She stepped away from Aarav and walked to the refreshment table, where she poured herself a glass of water. She sipped it slowly, trying to steady her nerves. She felt a hand on her shoulder and turned to see her sister, Kavya, standing behind her.

"Dee, you look stunning!" Kavya said, her eyes wide with admiration. "And, jiju is so caring."

Navya forced a smile, her heart heavy.

"Thank you, Kav. We're really happy."

Kavya smiled, but Navya could see the doubt in her eyes. She had always been perceptive, and Navya wondered if she could sense the tension.

"Are you sure everything is okay?" Kavya asked, her voice softening. "You seem... different tonight."

Navya's smile faltered, and she took a deep breath.

"It's just a bit overwhelming, you know? But everything is fine. Just getting used to married life."

Kavya nodded, but her eyes remained fixed on Navya with a concern that Navya couldn't ignore. She quickly changed the subject, talking about her latest fashion collection, Kavya's studies, and the upcoming projects she was working on. Kavya talked about everything excitedly, but she felt a pang of guilt for lying to her sister.

As the evening progressed, the room filled with more and more people. Friends, colleagues, and acquaintances all offered their best wishes, and Navya and Aarav played their roles to perfection. Aarav's PR team had them rehearse every interaction, from holding hands to only sticking to the topics that wouldn't put any of them in a difficult spot.

Soon, they were called back to the stage for a few speeches. Aarav stepped forward first, his voice steady and clear.

"Marriage is not just a celebration of two people, but the union of two families, two souls, and two destinies."

He paused, taking a deep breath, and then continued, his eyes never leaving Navya's face.

"Navya, your elegance is not just in the way you carry yourself, but in the way you create beauty through your designs. You see the world in a way that is both unique and profound, and it is this vision that has inspired me every day since we met. To be very honest, when I first met you, I wasn't sure whether it would work out, but your beauty, both inside and out made me believe in you."

Navya's cheeks flushed with a delicate pink, and she felt a warmth spread through her chest. She knew it was a speech written by the PR team, but she still felt good hearing him appreciate her.

"Your talent, Navya, is something that I admire deeply. But beyond your professional achievements, it is your grace and kindness that have captured my heart. You are not just a brilliant designer; you are a compassionate and caring individual, and I am the luckiest man in the world to call you my wife."

The audience erupted into applause, and Navya felt the tears welling up in her eyes. She wasn't sure if they were tears of joy or sorrow.

When it was her turn, Navya took the microphone, her hands trembling slightly. She looked out at the sea of faces, feeling a mix of emotions. She wanted to tell them the truth, to break down the facade and reveal the pain she was feeling. But she couldn't. She had to be strong, for everyone's sake. Aarav pressed her hands as he passed her the microphone and she looked up at him. His eyes were back to the indifferent, cold expression, but Navya could see the threat looming in them.

She swallowed the lump in her throat. She had been warned, but the reminder still stung. She wished, just for a moment, that he would look at her like he used to, with genuine affection and warmth. But those days were long gone, and the only thing left was this hollow charade.

"Thank you all for being here tonight," she began, her voice steady but filled with a warmth she hoped would mask her inner turmoil. "Aarav and I are deeply grateful for your presence and your blessings. We both believe marriage is a partnership, a journey we embark on together. And for us, it's a journey filled with love and respect."

She said what the PR team had written for her.

Aarav smiled. He raised his hand to take the microphone from her when Navya placed her hand on his extended one and looked into his eyes.

"Aarav, when I first heard about this marriage, I was apprehensive, unsure what to expect. But as we spent time together, I saw a man of great integrity and passion. Your dedication to your work, your respect for our traditions, and your unwavering kindness have made me feel secure."

Aarav looked at her, his heart raced. *This was not in the script.*

"Today, I stand here, not just as your wife, but as your partner and friend. I promise to stand by you in all your endeavours, to support you, and to be the person you can always turn to. Together, we will build a life that is as beautiful and meaningful as the designs we create and the spaces we inhabit."

As Navya's words echoed through the hall, the pretence that had bound them for so long began to unravel like a frayed thread in the wind. Aarav stood frozen, his perfectly composed facade cracking under the weight of her promise. It wasn't just a challenge to him; it was a *vow.* And Navya was never going to break it.

FOURTEEN
LONG ROAD AHEAD

The flashes of the reception hall still danced in Aarav's mind. He felt strangely hollow, like a meticulously crafted shell. He had delivered his lines - the perfectly rehearsed speech about Navya, her beauty, and her talent. It was a PR stunt, a performance for the gathered families and friends, an exercise in projecting an image. He hadn't meant a single word.

And then Navya had spoken. He didn't know why, but he felt like her words were genuine. The unwavering promise to stand by him all her life as his wife, it was a true promise. It was a blatant deviation from the script they had agreed on, or rather he had made her agree on. But her speech, so artless and yet honest, had threatened the very foundation he had built to keep her at bay. It had been a display of something he could neither comprehend nor tolerate.

The party ended in a joyous rush of goodbyes and wishes. He stood beside Navya, smiling mechanically, as guests trickled out. He could feel her presence next to him, a warmth that was both alien and oddly comforting.

When they retreated to their room, Navya entered the walk-in wardrobe, and Aarav moved towards the balcony, needing the cool night air for a moment. As he leaned over the railing, the weight of his charade pressed down on him. He was supposed to be a husband and a partner, but he felt like an imposter, trapped in a life he didn't want.

Aarav heard her footsteps, she was behind him. But he didn't turn.

"It's a beautiful night," she said, her voice soft.

He didn't respond. What was he supposed to say? That he wished, more than anything, that he wasn't there? That he wished she wasn't there? That he had never married her?

To his surprise, she didn't push for conversation. However, she moved closer, until she was standing right beside him. He could feel her warmth radiating onto his skin. She didn't look at him either, instead she just stared ahead at the city lights.

Then she did the most unexpected thing - she reached out and took his hand. Her fingers intertwined with his, sending a jolt he couldn't ignore. The touch was tentative yet possessive, a silent invitation. He should have pulled away, he knew it, but the warmth of her skin against his was unexpectedly grounding. He let her hold his hand.

The silence stretched between them, charged with an unspoken energy. Aarav stared at their joined hands, a sense of unreality washing over him. It was as if the facade they had both so carefully maintained was cracking. He looked at her, her eyes were on him too.

As she moved closer, her hand brushing his chest while she tried to take his tie off, an unexpected heat flared within him. It was just for a moment, a fraction of time, but it felt profoundly real and dangerous. It was completely unexpected.

Panic seized him. It was a calculated move, he told himself. She wanted to mend things, but he was not ready and would never be.

"Don't touch me," he snapped, his voice low and dangerous. "Don't you ever think you can just seduce me!" The words were harsh, even to his own ears, but he couldn't stop them.

Seduce? The word was like a slap on Navya's face. How could he possibly think that? The accusation was so far from the truth it was almost laughable, if it had not hurt so much. The pain was sharp, a raw, throbbing feeling in her chest.

This wasn't just a rejection; it was a complete misinterpretation of her intentions.

A wave of humiliation washed over her. She could see, in the harsh glare of his eyes, a reflection of her own perceived worthlessness.

A part of her, a small, fragile part, wanted to lash out, to hurl insults back at him, to make him feel the pain he had so carelessly inflicted upon her. But another part, the part that still clung to the faint hope in her heart, held her back.

As Navya watched him retreat, she felt the sting of tears prick at her eyes. She wasn't some scheming woman trying to trap him. She was simply trying to sort things out. But he seemed to perceive every gesture, every word as an attack, a manipulation. His words had cut deep, and the sincerity she expressed on stage felt like a foolish embarrassment. She wanted to scream, to lash out, but instead, she sat down on the edge of the bed, the perfect bride with a shattered heart.

The aroma drifted through the Singhania Mansion, a warm, inviting scent of spices and simmering vegetables that had been noticeably absent for the longest time. Navya, her hands dusted with flour, nervously adjusted the pallu of her saree. It was Sunday and this was her first attempt at cooking a proper meal for her new family, and the weight of expectations felt far heavier than the kadhai she'd been stirring. She didn't have any expectations from Aarav after last night of course, but she wanted to do it for her family who had welcomed and accepted her so warmly.

Aarav, who had been in his study, emerged with a frown. He glanced at Navya and then at the dining table, set with the dishes. He didn't say anything, but the way he crossed his arms and leaned against the doorway spoke volumes. He was ready to mock her, again. She would not take his words to heart, she decided and continued her work.

Aryan rushed out of the room, his eyes gleaming with anticipation.

"Wow, something actually smells good for a change!" he announced, giving Navya a wide smile. "Did you make this, Bhabhi?"

"Yes, Aryan," Navya replied, relieved by his enthusiasm. "I hope you like it."

Avni followed, her hair still wet from a shower. She perched on a chair and looked at the spread with a critical eye.

"It looks delicious, Bhabhi. Thank you for cooking," She added excitedly.

Navya smiled, a flicker of hope igniting within her.

The siblings started serving themselves, Aryan piling his plate high. He took a bite of the dal, his eyes widening.

"This is amazing, Bhabhi! Seriously, the best Dal I have had in ages!" He scooped up another spoonful, seemingly oblivious to the tension in the air.

Avni took a smaller portion, savoring each bite.

"It's really tasty!"

Navya's heart warmed, a genuine smile blooming on her face.

Aarav, meanwhile, remained silent, taking a small portion of each dish. He chewed slowly, his brow furrowed in concentration. Navya watched him, her heart beating a little faster. She could see the subtle shift in his expression and the way his eyes lingered on the food before he reluctantly took another bite.

"It's...okay," Aarav finally said, his voice flat. "The dal is a bit too rich in salt, and the vegetables could have been cooked a little more."

Navya's smile faltered. She knew he was deliberately trying to find flaws, but it still stung.

The younger siblings looked at each other.

"This is a hundred times better than that bland stuff Kanta Kaki cooks," Aryan frowned, looking at Aarav.

"Yes, Bhaiya. It tastes like home," Avni agreed and added, "I would love to learn from you, Bhabhi."

Aarav ignored them, continuing to eat his meal with an impassive expression. Beneath his facade of indifference, however, a different battle was being waged. He couldn't deny that the food was good.

He found himself taking a second serving, almost unconsciously. He tried to rationalize it, telling himself that he was simply filling his stomach, but deep down, he knew it was more than that. The food and the love that had gone into making it was reaching him despite his best efforts to shut it out.

As the meal progressed, the sound of chatter filled their dining room, a stark contrast to the silence that had been the norm. Aryan regaled Navya with stories of his college, and Avni spoke about the new design Navya had launched just before the wedding. Every now and then, Avni would ask Navya questions, further drawing her into the conversation. Aarav, despite his attempts to remain aloof, couldn't help but listen; a seed of curiosity was beginning to sprout within him.

After the meal, Navya supervised as the househelp, Robin cleaned the table. A sense of quiet accomplishment washed over her. She had created something, a shared experience that had, for a brief time, brought harmony to this fractured home. She knew it was a long road ahead, considering Aarav's indifference but for today, she would hold onto that small victory. And it was only the beginning.

FIFTEEN

Calculations and Cracks

The morning light, usually a welcome thing, felt harsh and accusing as it sliced through the gap in the curtains. Navya lay stiffly on the vast bed, the space beside her cold and empty, *as usual*. She had become accustomed to his early-morning disappearances, each one a tiny sting of rejection.

It had been three weeks since their wedding. Three weeks of strained smiles, forced conversations, and the heavy thud of unspoken words bouncing between them. They were supposed to be newlyweds, basking in the glow of a happy union, yet they felt like two strangers sharing the same roof.

Navya sighed, pulling the silk duvet closer. She traced the outline of the intricate henna on her palm, a faded reminder of the elaborate, joyful rituals that had culminated in this hollow reality. The wedding had been a spectacle, a seamless blend of traditions and extravagance, that was meticulously curated by their families. It was supposed to be the start of a love story, but it felt more like the beginning of a carefully scripted drama.

Despite the chasm between them, their PR team – a sleek, efficient operation headed by one Ms. Tanya Rao – had done a remarkable job of projecting a different image to the world. Their social media feeds were bursting with perfectly posed pictures: Navya and Aarav laughing over breakfast, Navya gazing adoringly at Aarav during a charity event, Aarav holding Navya's hand as they walked into a family function. Each photo was meticulously crafted, and designed to elicit envy and admiration.

Navya sometimes found herself scrolling through their feed, a strange mix of fascination and despair welling inside her. It was like looking at a parallel universe, a version of their lives that existed only in the digital ether. The comments were always the same - "Couple goals!" "So perfect together!" "Made for each other!" - each word a sharp contrast to the reality of her silent breakfasts and polite goodnights delivered from opposite ends of their enormous bedroom.

She finally dragged herself out of bed, her movements stiff and listless. As she headed downstairs, she heard the faint murmur of voices from the dining room. Aarav was already there, engrossed in a conversation with Tanya.

"...the engagement numbers are fantastic, Mr. Singhania," Tanya said. "The 'couple interview' is trending well. We should capitalize on this momentum. Perhaps a joint appearance on 'Morning Buzz' next week?"

Aarav nodded, his expression detached, his eyes flickering to Navya briefly as she entered.

"That sounds fine," he said, his voice devoid of warmth. He didn't even offer a 'good morning'.

Tanya turned to Navya, her smile bright and practiced.

"Good morning, Mrs. Singhania! You're looking lovely. Don't forget, we have a photoshoot at the vineyard this afternoon. It's important to continue showing that 'perfect harmony'."

Navya plastered a smile on her face, the practiced ease of the smile feeling strange in her mouth.

"Of course, Tanya," she replied, her voice perfectly neutral. "And you can call me Navya."

Aarav looked up at her but didn't say anything.

"Did the kids leave?" Navya asked Kanta.

"Yes, Avni had early school today, and Aryan had football practice," she replied as she served.

Navya sat down at the table while the staff silently served her breakfast – an assortment of fruits and yogurt, all perfectly arranged. Aarav picked up a slice of toast without making any eye contact.

"The charity gala is next weekend," Tanya continued, her voice crisp and businesslike. "We want to highlight your commitment to children's education. Mr. Singhania, we will need you to make a brief speech. Navya, we will focus on your interaction with the kids."

Navya nodded, feeling like a puppet being moved from one stage to another, her own thoughts and feelings irrelevant. She had become an accessory in her own life, a character in a play she hadn't even auditioned for. She glanced at Aarav, hoping for even a flicker of acknowledgment, but his attention was on his phone, his face an impenetrable mask.

The polished facade she was forced to maintain felt like a suffocating blanket. She longed for authenticity, a real conversation, and a chance to connect with the man she had married. She wondered how long they could continue living this lie, this precisely built meticulously crafted illusion of happiness. And she wondered with a pang of fear, if she could ever break free from this cage. The fear wasn't just for the charade, but for her own heart, slowly growing weary of the show.

The late afternoon sun slanted through the panoramic windows of their home studio, painting long shadows across the drafting table. Navya, perched on a tall stool, was draped in swathes of vibrant emerald silk, her brows furrowed in concentration. Aarav, on the other hand, stood at the table, his hands resting on a blueprint, his gaze locked on the architectural sketches. The air that usually buzzed with creative energy, now crackled with a silent tension.

"Aarav, are you even looking at this?" Navya finally asked, her voice sharper than she intended. She gestured impatiently with a pencil towards a mood board covered with fabric samples, sketches, and inspirational images.

"The pavilion needs to flow, to feel ephemeral, not...stiff."

Aarav sighed. He turned from the blueprint.

"Stiff? Navya, it's structurally sound. "The design employs a series of interconnected arches, creating a sense of openness and...geometry. It's not just about flowing fabric."

"But it is about fabric!" Navya retorted, throwing her head back. "The primary purpose of this project is to showcase the textile, to let it breathe. Your arches look like they're trying to imprison it! I need movement, lightness!"

The joint project - a textile pavilion commissioned for an upcoming contemporary art festival – had seemed like the perfect opportunity to partner the business.

Aarav ran a hand through his hair.

"Navya, you can't just drape silk on anything and expect it to stand. There are engineering principles involved! I can't just make arches bend and sway like...ribbons."

Suddenly, his phone rang.

"Hello?" he picked it up without looking at the caller ID.

"Mr. Singhania, you need to come to the school. Avni is facing potential suspension."

SIXTEEN

Avni in Trouble

Aarav slid into the driver's seat of his car, the principal's ominous phone call still ringing in his ears. He adjusted the rearview mirror, briefly scanning his features for any signs of weakness before he hit the ignition. He was about to pull out of the driveway when the passenger door swung open with a sharp thwack. He didn't need to look to know who it was.

"Navya," Aarav sighed, his voice low and tight.

She settled into the seat beside him. He deliberately avoided making eye contact, focusing instead on gripping the steering wheel tighter than necessary.

"What are you doing?" he asked in a flat tone.

Navya didn't miss a beat, her voice as unwavering as the stare she fixed on him.

"I am going to Avni's school."

His grip on the steering wheel tightened.

"Absolutely not," he retorted, his voice sharper now. "This has nothing to do with you. It's a family matter."

He felt the familiar surge of frustration build inside him, a bitter cocktail of resentment and anger. Why couldn't she just stay out of it? He had always been fiercely protective of the limited family he had, and he regarded Navya as an intrusion.

Navya's gaze didn't waver, her lips pressed into a thin line, and he hated the defiant spark he saw in her eyes.

"Avni *is* my family, Aarav. I am not about to sit here while she possibly gets suspended. I am her older sister-in-law. She is family."

"She is my sister and this is my problem. I don't need your interference," Aarav growled, his knuckles white against the dark leather. "This is not a field trip."

"If you remember you made me her guardian, legally just a few days before our wedding. And I am telling you, I am going," she countered, her voice firm, laced with a controlled intensity that was infuriating him. She looked him directly in the eye, her expression unyielding. "With you or without you, Aarav. I have my own car."

He stared at her for a long moment, his jaw clenched. He hated this. He absolutely loathed the situation he had gotten himself into. He had, in a moment of what he now recognized as utter naivete, appointed Navya as Avni's legal guardian. He had thought it was the right thing to do, a responsible decision. Often, when he had been too busy with some project, he had missed Avni's parent-teacher meetings or Annual Day function. He thought Navya could fill in those duties. if only he had known the truth a few days before.

And now, because of his past foolishness, he was stuck.

He looked at Navya with furious eyes but he could see the determination in her eyes, the same stubbornness he had initially found so alluring but now found absolutely unbearable. He knew she meant it. She would visit the school with, or without him.

He let out a frustrated sigh, the sound heavy in the small space of the car.

"Fine," he conceded, his voice laced with a barely contained rage. "But don't expect me to hold your hand or introduce you as my wife there. You're just... a spectator."

Navya said nothing, but a glimmer of satisfaction flashed in her eyes. She fastened her seatbelt, her gaze fixed ahead, and settled into her seat as if nothing had happened.

The rest of the drive to Avni's school was conducted in a tense silence, the only thing that made a sound was the engine and the occasional nervous tap of Aarav's fingers against the steering wheel. He could feel Navya's presence like a physical weight, the scent of her perfume filling the car, a suffocating reminder of their fractured relationship. He hated that she was forcing her way in.

He glanced at her out of the corner of his eye. Her face was a mask of composure, but he could see the faint tremor in her hands and they were clasped tightly in her lap. She was genuinely concerned about Avni,. he realised. It didn't make him less angry, though, just more perplexed.

The school gates loomed ahead, a stark contrast to the bright, sunshine-yellow exterior. The building seemed to press down on him, the weight of the situation settling heavily on his shoulders. He pulled into a parking spot, the engine sputtering to a stop.

Aarav got out of the car first, not waiting for Navya, not wanting to acknowledge her, his long strides carrying him towards the front entrance. Navya followed close behind, her quiet presence like a shadow that he couldn't shake off. He still didn't want her there, but deep down, he had a feeling this might just get a whole lot more complicated.

When they entered the principal's office, they saw Mr. Sharma, a stern-faced man in his late fifties, sitting behind a large oak desk. Facing him was Avni, tears in her eyes.

"Avni!" Navya rushed to hug her. "What happened, baby?"

Mr. Sharma cleared his throat.

"This is a serious matter, Mrs Navya. She has been caught with a love letter, exchanged during school hours... It's a clear violation of school policy. Suspension is the standard disciplinary action."

Avni's eyes prick with tears and she looks down at her hands, twisting them in her lap.

"With all due respect, Principal Sharma," Navya interjected, her voice calm but firm, "I understand the school policy, but I believe we should look at the context here. Avni is a bright student, and this is clearly an isolated incident."

Principal Sharma raised an eyebrow.

"Are you suggesting we disregard school rules?"

Aarav turned towards Navya, his voice stern.

"Navya, this isn't your place. I can handle this."

He glanced at Avni, a flicker of disappointment in his eyes. Navya watched him, her brow furrowed slightly.

"I said before, Avni is my family too. And I think we have to look at the situation from her point of view. It's a tender age. Perhaps instead of punishment, we can focus on understanding what's going on with her, and make sure that she is comfortable conveying her feelings. We can make sure this does not happen again. Isn't it our responsibility to guide her, Principal Sir?"

"Guidance is one thing, Mrs. Singhania," Mr Sharma responded, his voice laced with skepticism, "but this letter clearly demonstrates a lack of discipline. It disrupts the school environment."

"Disrupts?" Navya questioned, her brow furrowing slightly. "A letter expressing a teenage crush disrupts the school environment?" She paused, taking a deep breath. "I understand the need for rules and discipline, Principal Sharma, but there has to be space for empathy, too. We need to guide these children, not punish them for being human."

The older man remained silent for a moment before speaking again.

"You've given this some thought, haven't you?"

Navya nodded, "I have. I believe in second chances. And I think Avni needs our support and understanding, not a punishment that might set her back further emotionally and academically."

Aarav stared at Navya, surprised. He hadn't expected her to intervene, let alone challenge the principal. He didn't know how to react to this. He finally uncrossed his arms and took a step forward.

"She's right, Principal Sharma. Avni is one of the most disciplined girls I know and she wouldn't do anything intentionally to disrupt the school," He spoke to the Principal but his gaze shifted to Navya for a brief moment, a flicker of acknowledgement reflected in his usually indifferent eyes.

"Perhaps," Principal Sharma conceded after a long pause, his tone slightly softer, "we can consider a warning instead of immediate suspension. However, Avni will have to be more careful in the future and understand the importance of following rules. If I see any other such thing as this, it means she is not learning her lesson, and I will not show any more leniency. You understand, Avni?"

Avni just nodded.

"Would you like to meet with the school counselor and figure out a way to deal with it?" the principal asked Aarav and Navya.

"Yes," both of them said in unison.

Aarav looked at Navya. Her actions had rattled him.

His siblings had always been drawn to Navya, even though he tried to keep them at arm's length from her. He could never understand why. If they started seeking her out, confiding in her, and becoming close to her, that would complicate things. They would be hurt when they met the cunning woman hiding behind their adorable sister-in-law.

Aarav clenched his jaw. He would make sure they didn't get too attached to her. Maybe a carefully placed word here, a manufactured disagreement there, anything to remind them. He wouldn't let her become a part of his family simply by being... kind. He needed to retain control. He needed to be the one who called the shots, and he wouldn't let Navya gain this unexpected leverage with his innocent siblings. He would find ways to ensure they didn't get too close to her, even if he had to create a wedge between them himself.

SEVENTEEN
HOPE FOR TOMORROW

"Hope for Tomorrow"

Aarav looked at the banner held up at the entrance of the Children's Education Gala. He always donated to children's causes. But, it was the first time he was doing it to show off. He entered the hall followed by Navya.

The air was filled with the gentle murmur of polite conversation, punctuated by the occasional delighted squeal of a child being introduced to a celebrity guest or admiring a particularly sparkly decoration. Several large screens displayed images of children benefiting from the charity's work, subtly tugging at the heartstrings of the attendees.

As soon as Aarav and Navya entered, they immediately drew the attention of the assembled guests and the press photographers. Their smiles were radiant, their body language carefully calibrated to project an image of effortless affection. They moved smoothly through the area, shaking hands with dignitaries and donors.

Navya moved through the children's area with practiced ease. She knelt beside a young girl struggling with a glitter glue stick, her own smile bright and encouraging. She asked about the girl's drawing, offered gentle suggestions, and even managed to fashion a passable glitter butterfly out of a spare paper template. The photos being snapped by the ever-present photographer would be perfect for tomorrow's glossy magazines. Navya, the nurturing, involved wife. Another win for their fabricated narrative.

Aarav scanned the place, searching for Navya. He didn't realize where she went while he was talking to a business associate. He saw a gaggle of children gathered around in a corner. He walked towards them only to see Navya, sitting on the ground with the children. He watched as she laughed at a silly joke, her head thrown back, her eyes sparkling. For a moment, a flicker of something real sparked within him, a forgotten echo of the woman he had once wanted to spend his life with.

He cleared his throat, the sound a little too loud for the gentle atmosphere. Navya looked up, her smile faltering slightly as her gaze met his.

"The committee is asking for us," he said, "They would like to thank us for our donation."

Navya straightened, the easygoing warmth in her eyes replaced with a cool reserve. She gave the children a final, warm hug.

"Alright."

As she walked towards him, leading him away from the children, she kept her, head held high, her smile still in place.

"You could have waited, Aarav. I was having fun with the kids," Navya hissed, under her breath.

Aarav's calmness vanished, quickly replaced with a forced composure.

"That's what I don't want," he replied, keeping his voice low and even. "To let you have a good time, remember? Moreover, today's entire point was to show them that we are a united front, a power couple, not two bickering children. So stop it."

"A united front? Is that what we are?" Navya's voice was cutting. "I am fed up, Aarav. I am tired of playing a part in this charade."

They had reached a quieter corner of the lawn. The photography team, thankfully, was currently occupied photographing another donor.

"We decided, Navya," Aarav said, his voice rising slightly in frustration.

"Not we, you decided," Navya reminded, her eyes blazing. "I never agreed to this."

Aarav opened his mouth to argue, but the words caught in his throat. He could see the weariness in her eyes, the genuine pain that he wanted to see.

"Don't you realize, Aarav?" Navya continued, her voice trembling slightly. "It's not the public that we're fooling. It's us. We're fooling ourselves into believing that we can live like this, pretending everything is perfect when we're falling apart. Is this what you wanted?"

"No, Navya," he said in a plain tone. "I wanted us to be a couple, actually happy. But you didn't leave me a choice."

He turned to leave but stopped when she held his arm. Aarav looked at her hand on his arm for a second and then brushed it off with force. He left without glancing back at her. Oblivious to the fact that few cameras had captured them from a distance.

Aarav felt a knot tighten in his gut as he scrolled through the endless stream of news articles. His face, frozen in a fleeting moment of irritation, was plastered across every screen, next to a headline screaming about his supposed mistreatment of Navya. He ran a frustrated hand through his hair. It was a disaster, precisely the kind of public spectacle he had desperately tried to avoid.

Yes, he had brushed her hand away. Perhaps more forcefully than he had intended.

He wanted to see a flicker of hurt in her eyes, a sign that she understood the boundaries he desperately wanted her to acknowledge. But he hadn't wanted this. He hadn't imagined it would be filmed, dissected, and broadcast for the world to see.

The negative publicity was a catastrophe. His reputation, carefully cultivated over years, was now taking a hit. The very people he needed to impress were now seeing him as a callous, uncaring husband. This, he knew, could impact his deals, his brand, everything.

He hadn't wanted to hurt her publicly, to damage her image, or to create this media circus. His intention had been purely personal, a private jab meant for her ears and her experience, not the world's judgement. Now, he had to navigate the fallout, carefully crafting a response that wouldn't further damage his image. The whole thing was a delicate balancing act, one he desperately wished he could undo. He had wanted to inflict an emotional wound, not a public relations nightmare. And now, he had to figure out how to salvage what remained.

The sleek, modern conference room felt like a pressure cooker. Aarav sat at the head of the table, jaw tight, his usual cool demeanor cracking under the weight of the past few months. Across from him, Navya was fidgeting with her phone. Around them, the PR team, led by the ever-composed Ms. Tanya Rao, looked like they were preparing for a high-stakes chess match.

"So, to reiterate," Tanya said, her voice smooth as polished marble, "this is a serious issue, Mr. Singhania."

Aarav's fingers drummed on the table, a restless rhythm that mirrored the unease churning inside him. He knew it was true. The carefully constructed image of marital bliss was crumbling, revealing the uncomfortable truth of their arrangement. The public saw it and it might also create a loss in his business. He could lose contracts. He had built his empire on precision, and control, and this situation felt like a runaway train.

"So, what's the plan, exactly?" he asked, his voice clipped.

Tanya smiled a practiced, professional smile that didn't quite reach her eyes.

"The plan is to reframe the narrative. We have two ways. First, a Public Apology and Explanation; a televised interview or a carefully worded statement where you express genuine remorse. But you wouldn't explicitly admit guilt," she said, opening her tablet. "You could say something like you deeply regret that your actions were misinterpreted. It was never intended was never to cause Navya any discomfort, you could say you were distracted or tired."

"Hmm," Aarav said thoughtfully. "And the other?"

"Other way, if the Mrs speaks out," Tanya said and Navya's head snapped up. "a carefully drafted statement."

"Like?"

"Navya could release a statement," Tanya explained. "Saying that she was not upset, that it was a minor incident, or that she even found it amusing, and that the media is creating a problem where none exists."

Aarav took a deep breath. He knew his personal life would dictate the success of his business, that is why he had hired a PR agency, still it felt humiliating . The coldness with which he had treated Navya was now reflecting badly on him. But the idea of staging a fight, of turning their private battle into public theatre, felt like a betrayal of some kind, even if their marriage was already a performance.

He looked at Navya. Her expression was a mix of apprehension and confusion.

"What do you think, Navya?" he asked, his voice softer than he intended.

"Since when did you start asking for my suggestions?" she asked with a frown.

"I don't want you to mess things up like you always do," he taunted.

"I mess up?" Her voice was low, dangerously controlled. "Aarav, don't you understand? This isn't just about your image. It's about the image I have also protected since the beginning of my career. Everyone saw the clips. Everyone's talking. My family, our friends, the media."

"And they all think I am a detached, uncaring husband." Aarav ran his hand through his already disheveled hair.

"And I, a helpless wife who tolerates her husband's useless tantrums!"

Aarav flinched, the truth of her words hitting him. He had always been fiercely protective of their image and their privacy. This felt like a betrayal of everything they had built.

"I didn't mean to." The words felt flimsy even to his own ears.

Navya laughed, a bitter, humorless sound.

"Really? I don't believe you. For someone so concerned with appearances, you sure have a funny way of showing it. My entire reputation got dragged through the mud with you!"

"Don't blame this on me, Navya! You started it. Your reputation is almost princess-like. Maybe you should try being a little less perfect and come back to earth!" he shot back, the frustration finally bubbling over. He hated that she was making him feel like a failure.

Her eyes widened, a hurt that seemed deeper than anger flickering briefly across her face.

"You're deflecting, Aarav," Navya said, her voice dangerously calm. "This was never about me. I never wanted this. You dragged me into this Social Media PR nonsense!"

"Excuse me!" Tanya interrupted, not liking a jab at her job.

Both of them looked at her. They didn't realize they were in the office, and the PR team was present.

"Tanya, you may leave now," Aarav said. "I'll call you later."

Tanya gathered her stuff and left the room while glaring at Navya.

"If the media has ruined it, the PR will rectify it," Aarav said to Navya. "We don't need to play the blame game here."

"Fine then, do what your PR says. But remember, I won't be a part of it. I will not release any statement from my side. Because honestly, I am tired of pretending everything is okay when it is not."

She turned on her heels and walked out, leaving behind a confused Aarav.

EIGHTEEN
THE GIFT

Navya stared at the spreadsheet on her laptop, the numbers blurring into an indistinguishable mass. She had been replaying the argument with Aarav in her head.

A gentle knock on the door jolted Navya back to reality. She looked up, surprised to see Megha standing at the door with a hesitant smile. Megha was a warm, cheerful presence, a stark contrast to the grey mood Navya had been inhabiting lately.

"Hey, hope I am not interrupting," Megha said, her voice filled with concern. "I was in the area for some work and thought I'd pop in to say hello."

Navya smiled genuinely at her.

"Megha! It's good to see you. Please, come in," she gestured towards the small visitor's chair in front of her desk.

Megha settled down, immediately noticing that Navya seemed upset.

"Everything alright? You look... a little lost."

Navya sighed and closed her laptop. She was usually guarded about her personal life at work, but with Megha, she felt a strange urge to unburden herself. Her voice trembled as she recounted the silent torment she was enduring.

"I don't understand, Megha," she whispered, tears welling in her eyes. "It's like he despises me. I try so hard, but nothing I do is ever good enough. I feel so alone."

Megha listened patiently. She had a hint of all this after seeing the video surfacing online. She knew Aarav, he would never even think of hurting someone like this. Something was clearly wrong. She could see the pain in Navya's eyes, the hurt that slowly chipped away at her vibrant spirit.

"He... he doesn't even acknowledge me most of the time," Navya continued, her voice cracking. "I feel like I am invisible to him. Like I am just... a ghost in his life."

Megha reached across the table and squeezed Navya's hand.

"I won't say I understand, Navya," Megha said softly. "Because I don't. But I know he cares. He can be terrible at showing it, though."

"It's more than that. Do you know Aarav deliberately hurts me?" Navya said, her voice cracking slightly. "He wants to make my life hell. He said that to my face."

Megha couldn't believe her ears. *Aarav had really said that?*

"Navya, all this... is confusing me. But don't worry. I'll talk to Aarav."

"No," Navya said. "I want to understand him myself. I think I can handle this, Megha, I'll figure it out."

"I know you are strong, and you'll tame that beast." Navya laughed and Megha relaxed a little seeing her smile.

But Megha knew that simply comforting Navya wasn't enough. She had to understand what had caused this sudden, dramatic shift in Aarav's behavior.

Aarav stared at his reflection, the arguments with Navya flashed in his mind. She had been fierce, protecting her image that she had built was getting questioned. But wasn't it something he wanted? To ruin her?

Moreover, the PR team had suggested a statement from Navya. He understood the logic, in a way. It was all calculated, a performance designed to appease public opinion. But Navya's outburst was something that made his stomach clench.

He remembered how Navya's eyes had blazed with frustration and hurt when he had agreed to the PR's idea.

He knew it was all his strategy from the beginning but he didn't want their image destroyed. He just wished there was a way to do it without feeling like a complete pawn in his own game. He hesitated, the carefully crafted narrative of their lives feeling heavier than ever. He wasn't sure how they would recover from this, and the thought was terrifying.

He moved across the room running his hand on his already disheveled hair, in frustration.

And his eyes fell on it. On a gift box. It was wrapped and kept on the shelf. He had seen it in Navya's hand on their wedding night. Maybe she had wanted to give it to him. He cautiously pulled the box down, the paper crinkling slightly under his fingers. He hesitated momentarily, a strange mix of curiosity and apprehension swirling within him. A sticker over it that read - ***"A small gift to help you stay connected to me, mostly ;)".***

Aarav chuckled. He couldn't help clicking a picture of it. Aarav carefully unwrapped the present. A sleek, black box was revealed, printed with the logo of a tech company he admired.

He carefully opened it to reveal a collection of gadgets – wireless headphones, a sleek smartwatch, an external hard drive, a streaming device, a wireless power bank, and an E-reader. It was a tech enthusiast's dream, and Aarav was nothing if not a tech enthusiast. He couldn't help but smile.

He had been researching headphones for weeks, and the power bank, a constant bane of his travel life, was a perfect solution. Navya, it seemed, had been paying attention after all.

He held the headphones and turned them over, admiring the gift. It was a thoughtful gift, he couldn't deny that, even if the timing felt off. The anger was still there, a dull ache beneath the surface, but it was starting to be challenged, little by little, by a reluctant appreciation.

He couldn't help himself. Reaching for his phone, and with a small hint of gratitude, arranged the gadgets carefully on the cover of a magazine.

"When your amazing wife knows you better than you know yourself. Time to become a tech wizard, Thank you so much Mrs for the thoughtful gift!"

Aarav captioned the Instagram story, the words pouring out of him in a rush of... well, he wasn't entirely sure what they were a rush of. He hadn't even cross checked with his PR team, hitting "Post" with a reckless abandon that surprised even himself.

Navya's fingers tightened around the steering wheel as the horn of the car in front of her blared. The traffic was a gridlock of red brake lights and frustrated sighs, and her day was quickly turning into a similar mess. She had been looking forward to getting home, to maybe having a quiet evening after a particularly draining day at work. Instead, her phone was buzzing insistently, a barrage of WhatsApp and Instagram notifications breaking the silence of her car.

There were many messages from Kavya too, she opened them and found a list of articles.

"Aarav and Navya: Back on Track?"

"Is the Public Spat a Sham?"

"Gadgets of Love: Decoding Aarav's Cryptic Post."

Confused, she opened Instagram and checked her tags.

It was Aarav's post, that sickeningly sweet, picture-perfect image of him holding up the tech gadget set she had wanted to gift to him.

So this was what the PR team came up with as an alternative. *To make a mockery of her first gift for Aarav.*

She had refused to give a statement, but wasn't it easier for Aarav to give a public interview and apologize? No - his ego was greater than an apology to her.

She read the caption. It was filled with gratitude to his "amazing wife," for the "thoughtful gift."

It wasn't the heartfelt response she had envisioned when she had carefully wrapped the gift. It was a calculated PR move, a flimsy bandage slapped over the gaping wound of their strained marriage.

Navya's grip on the steering wheel tightened further. The carefully planned evening she had envisioned was now a distant memory. The idea of going home to perform this ridiculous charade alongside Aarav, to smile for the cameras and pretend everything was fine, but this was something she couldn't bear. She closed the windows of the car and let out a scream. The warmth she had felt when she chose the gift had been replaced with a cold, hard feeling of being used. The gift, meant to signify a new beginning, was now a prop in Aarav's theater of public image management. And the worst part was, she knew she would have to play along.

♡♡♡

NINETEEN

WHISPERS IN THE HALLWAYS

Navya entered the room in passionate anger. Her eyes were red and her nostrils flared. Aarav was lying on the bed, scrolling through his phone with a smile on his face. That smile made her more furious.

She walked towards the bed and slammed her phone towards him, gaining his attention.

"You are back," Aarav said as he looked up, his smile still lingering.

"You posted it," Navya stated, her voice dangerously low. It wasn't a question.

Aarav's brow furrowed.

"Yeah, because I really appreciate it."

"Appreciate it?" Navya scoffed. "Come on, just be honest enough to accept that this is another PR stunt."

His smile was replaced with a confused scowl.

"What? Seriously? I posted it because I liked it, Navya!" He held up his phone, showing her the post. "I genuinely wanted to thank you."

"Oh, 'genuinely'," she mocked, mimicking his tone. "You really think I believe that? You wouldn't even post our photos without running it by the PR team! But this, something actually meaningful, you just... you are making fun of my first gift to you!"

The accusation stung. Aarav's voice rose in response, mirroring her anger.

"You think I only do things for PR?" He stood up, mirroring her posture, a challenge in his eyes. "You think I am incapable of genuine emotion?"

"I don't know what to think anymore," Navya admitted, the edge in her voice wavering, replaced by a flicker of hurt. The fact that she hadn't thought of this as a genuine moment for him, stung a little.

Aarav's anger seemed to deflate a touch at the shift in her tone. He ran a hand through his hair.

"Look, I made a mistake by posting it out there, but I couldn't... I just really liked the gift."

His unscripted honesty, took her aback. It was unlike the carefully crafted persona she knew. She looked at him and saw not the media-savvy architect but a man with honesty in his eyes. And there, in the tense silence, a strange, unfamiliar sensation bubbled in her chest, a tightening that was both unsettling and electrifying.

He had been angry at her a lot of times, but his anger today somehow raced her heartbeat.

She bit her lip, her eyes flickering down to his jawline.

"Okay," she whispered, the word barely audible. She needed to get out of the room to escape the confusing current that was pulling her under.

She turned abruptly and headed towards the balcony, the cool night air, a stark contrast to the heat that had suddenly filled the room. Aarav watched her go, his own confusion mirroring hers. He hadn't expected this reaction. He hadn't expected... anything, really. He had simply felt a wave of gratitude, and his instinct had been to share it. Now, he was left only frustrated. This woman didn't deserve gratitude, but exactly what he felt for her - *hatred.*

The gadgets lay on the bedside table, a silent testament to a night that had been anything but simple. The gift, intended as a gesture of connection, had instead sparked different firecrackers on both sides.

The scent of ginger and cardamom filled the house, a blanket woven by Navya's early morning efforts. She was at the stove, preparing tea. Her dark hair was pulled back in a messy bun, a few strands escaping to frame her face.

Aarav shuffled into the kitchen a few moments later, ready for office. He didn't look at her directly, instead headed straight for the breakfast table and collapsed into his usual chair.

Navya placed the fresh tea in front of him, and went back to the kitchen to help Kanta with breakfast. This was their usual morning routine, one of many routines they had awkwardly fallen into since their wedding.

“Bhai, can you help me fix this?” Aryan burst into the room, thrusting a battered skateboard towards Aarav. “The wheel’s all wobbly.”

Aarav set down his tea and took the skateboard. Navya watched, a gentle warmth spreading through her chest. She had heard stories from his cousins and relatives about Aarav’s protectiveness of his younger siblings, but this was the first time she was witnessing it firsthand. He might be aloof with her, but he clearly cared deeply for his family.

For the fifteen minutes, Aarav was completely engrossed in fixing the skateboard while Aryan provided a running commentary on his adventures with it. Navya, watching from the sidelines, felt a pang of longing. She wanted that easy camaraderie, that unguarded affection.

“Done!” Aarav said in satisfaction and Aryan grabbed his board and grinned at his brother.

"Thanks, Bhai! You’re the best."

Aarav ruffled his hair, his lips curving into a smile. It was a smile Navya had never seen directed her way.

“Be careful, idiot,” he said, his voice gruff but gentle.

“Good morning, Bhaiya!” Avni squealed, launching herself at Aarav, nearly knocking him off his chair.

Aarav caught her easily, a soft laugh escaping his lips.

“Easy there, you little tornado,” he chuckled.

“Good morning, Bhabhi,” she said to Navya as she placed a bowl of cereal in front of her.

Navya smiled and watched the siblings, they were chatting, sharing the details of their previous day, teasing each other in between. She had seen this side of Aarav before, but these glimpses of gentleness and affection are reserved solely for his family now. It was a stark contrast to the aloofness he displayed towards her since marriage, and yet, it offered a small beacon of promise.

“Kanta, bring Navya’s breakfast too,” Aarav said as Navya served Aryan. “She skips breakfast when she has important meetings.”

Navya looked at him, surprised. But he didn’t look at her, kept eating his food. He had noticed.

She sat beside him as Kanta served her.

“Thank you, she said, her voice barely above a whisper.

Aarav shrugged, not meeting her gaze.

Even though he didn’t say anything, her heart fluttered. It was like a tiny seed of hope planted in the fertile ground of her heart. It wasn’t the grand thing, but it was a sign, faint as the morning light, that perhaps, just perhaps, he cared. And for Navya, that was enough for now.

At night, Navya finished supervising the final kitchen deeds and walked directly to Aryan's room. She had seen him during dinner, he wasn't feeling well. She knocked on the door.

"Aryan?" Her voice was gentle and concerned.

"It's open, Bhabhi," she heard his weak voice followed by a cough.

Entering the room, she was welcomed with a discarded packet of cough drops on his desk, a testament to the battle Aryan was waging against a cold that had chosen the worst possible time to strike – right in the middle of his semester exams.

Aryan lay on his bed, a jumble of blankets barely disguising the fact that he hadn't changed into his night clothes.

"Do you have a fever, Aryan?" she asked as she sat beside him, touching his forehead.

He shook his head, the movement sending another stab of pain through his temples.

"Not yet," he managed to say. "But I might. I am having a headache like it's going to burst."

"I'll make you ginger tea with honey, just two minutes." She said and walked out after putting the duvet over him properly.

She walked towards the kitchen and started making tea.

"Navya?" It was Aarav's voice.

She was startled. His voice usually tinged with a cool disinterest when addressing her, held a hint of urgency now. He rarely called her name with such directness.

"You want something?" Navya asked, continuing her work.

He frowned, his brow furrowing slightly.

"No, I just checked on Avni and was going to check on Aryan. But why are you making tea now? We just had dinner," he noticed her hands were shaking slightly. Something was definitely off.

Navya took a deep breath, her gaze dropping to the floor for a moment before looking back at him.

"It's Aryan. He's not feeling well. He might have caught a fever, he is complaining of head and body aches."

Aarav didn't wait for another second and entered Aryan's room. A low moan escaped Aryan's lips as he shifted restlessly in bed. This wasn't just a normal sniffle.

“How are you feeling, buddy?” Aarav asked, ruffling his brother’s hair.

Aryan shook his head, unable to reply.

“I noticed it earlier this evening,” Navya replied softly as she walked inside holding the cup of tea.

“Does he have medicines?” Aarav walked towards the drawer beside the bed.

He opened it to see Aryan’s box of medicines. He stared at Navya with questioning eyes.

She answered his unasked question, "I usually refill it during my weekly grocery visit."

He had noticed it before, her care for his siblings. But he had never really acknowledged it.

"Has he taken medicine yet?" He asked.

“He has taken some cold compress and cough syrups,” then she helped Aryan sit. “Come on, drink this, you’ll feel better.”

“I still have most of the syllabus left, Bhabhi,” he said as he took the mug. “Thank you.”

"Don’t mention it, silly," she replied, smoothing his hair back from his forehead. "You are going to do the paper well, don’t push yourself too hard. You need to rest. Exams aren’t worth making yourself sick."

"But...they’re important," he protested, his voice raspy. “I need to..." he trailed off, unable to articulate the pressure he felt.

Navya’s hand stilled on his head.

“I know they’re important, Aryan. But your health is even more important. Your brother and I are both worried sick seeing you like this. Trust me, a few marks aren’t going to define you. Just take the day off. You can catch up when you’re feeling better."

“She is right, Aryan,” Aarav said, placing a hand on Aryan’s shoulder. The touch was comforting. "Health comes first.”

“I just...I don’t want to miss the exams.”

Aarav squeezed his shoulder.

“Hey, it’s okay. I understand. But rest is crucial. The textbooks can wait. I am sure you know more than you think. Just focus on getting better first.”

"Okay," Aryan whispered, his eyes closing. "Okay, I’ll rest. You both should sleep now, I am fine.”

“I am here,” both Navya and Aarav said together and then looked at each other.

"You don't need to," Aryan said, touched with his Bhai and Bhabhi's concern. "I'll call you if I need something. And I heard you both have an important meeting tomorrow. Good night."

Even though both of them wanted to stay with him, none of them argued about it.

"Fine," Aarav said. "We'll leave after you fall asleep."

The sterile white walls of the meeting room felt suffocating. Aarav had been waiting for Navya for two hours. The clients had arrived, and he and Navya were going to present the project together. Just as he was about to start the presentation, he saw her walk in.

"I am sorry, I am late," Navya apologized, panting.

She stood beside Aarav and pulled the laptop to herself.

"Were you trying to sabotage me?" Aarav whispered, his words sharp and cold.

She looked up at him. She had poured her heart and soul into this presentation, staying up late for days, refining every detail. And now, he was accusing her of trying to ruin it. But she pushed away the hurt, focusing on maintaining a veneer of composure.

"I would never intentionally compromise this project. You know how important it is to me too."

"You were late!" he accused.

"There was a reason," she said, not looking at him. "But you would only see it as another manipulation tactic."

She turned to the investors, a forced smile plastered on her face.

"Shall we start?"

The rest of the presentation was a blur. They presented together and answered questions but Navya's responses were automatic and mechanical. Inside, a storm was raging. How could he even think she would sabotage this project?

As the investors filed out after the meeting, murmurs of polite encouragement and thinly veiled concern hanging in the air, the room slowly emptied. Navya remained rooted to the spot, her gaze fixed on the intricate pattern of the carpet. She could feel his eyes on her, a burning intensity that was devoid of any warmth.

"I could have lost this project because of you!"

The accusation, so baseless, so cruel, finally broke through the daze she was in. Tears welled in her eyes, blurring her vision. She wanted to explain, wanted him to understand. But whatever she said, he would only see it as another manipulation tactic.

"Did you even bother to ask why? Did you even think, for a moment, that I could have a genuine reason for being late? Or am I just some villain in your story?" Her voice cracked, and the control she had so desperately clung to crumbled.

He turned away, his gaze fixed on the city skyline outside his window.

"You were late. The investors saw it. This presentation could be ruined because of you, because of your carelessness."

"I am not careless," she frowned. "But if you think I am, then good for you," She was tired of explaining herself to him all the time. "Now, if you'll excuse me, I have work to do."

She left while Aarav kept looking at her till she vanished from his sight.

Aarav returned home earlier than usual that evening. The stress of even the smallest chance of losing the deal was making him restless, he was unable to work. He looked at the watch, 5:30 PM. It was the earliest he had ever come back home.

"Bhai!" he saw Aryan running towards him with a bag on his shoulder. "Where is Bhabhi?" Aryan asked, his face alight with genuine joy.

"I don't know," he replied, confused. "She left for the boutique immediately after the meeting, but it's almost her time to be back. How are you feeling now? Why are you so happy?"

"I'll tell Bhabhi first," he said.

"Is Bhabhi home?" Aryan asked Kanta who opened the door for them. Without waiting for an answer, he dashed through the living room.

"Aryan," Navya walked out of her room. "How did it go?"

"Bhabhi!" he exclaimed, hugging her tightly. "Thank you, thank you, thank you! I don't know what I would have done without you!"

Navya was taken aback by his sudden outburst. But a small smile finally broke through her gloom.

He pulled back, his eyes shining.

"Thank you so much for coming into our life, Bhabhi. You took care of me the whole night! You were so patient. You even helped me go through my notes for the exam. I studied so much more because of you! I am sure I have aced the paper! I will definitely get good marks. Thank you," He took her hand and squeezed it.

Navya's heart warmed at his words. Even after Aryan had told her and Aarav to go to bed, she had stayed up with him. She coaxed him to drink fluids, and helped him prepare for the exam.

"Thank God the exam was in the afternoon, or I would have been finished!" he let out a dramatic sigh. "Oh, did you reach the meeting on time? We were still going through the study materials at dawn."

Aarav stood frozen just inside the doorway, watching the interaction. The confusion on his face was quickly replaced by guilt.

"Everything went well. Are you feeling better now?" Navya asked, her voice gentle.

"Much better, all thanks to you!" Aryan smiled at her. "I am going to study for the exam I have tomorrow. I'll come to you if I have doubts," He beamed at her again before rushing inside his room.

"Don't strain yourself," Navya smiled at him.

Then she looked at the doorway, her eyes meeting Aarav. His gaze was no longer cold. He opened his mouth as if to speak, but no words came. He looked away, guilt etching deep lines around his eyes.

The silence between them hung heavy, thick with unspoken words and complex emotions. Navya didn't know what to say, but her heart was filled with hope and apprehension. Had Aryan's simple act of gratitude finally pierced through Aarav's hardened exterior? Or was this just a fleeting moment, a temporary shift in his perception?

She walked into the room, leaving him standing in the doorway, staring at the floor, his inner turmoil evident in the tightening of his jaw. The weight of his accusations now seemed to press down on him. The seeds of doubt, planted by Aryan's innocent praise, had begun to sprout, and, for the first time, Aarav had to confront not only his actions but also the possibility that he might be terribly, terribly wrong.

TWENTY

The Nighmare

The bedside lamp cast a soft, amber glow, barely piercing the shadows that clung to the corners of the room. Navya stirred, a subtle shift in the mattress pulling her from the comfortable depths of slumber. Her eyes flickered open, landing on Aarav.

He wasn't asleep.

He was sitting upright, his back straight, breathing ragged and shallow.

Her heart skipped a beat, a strange mix of shock and bewilderment washing over her. She blinked, trying to dispel the image, wondering if she was still dreaming. But no, Aarav was still there, his silhouette outlined by the dim light of the lamp.

Navya's mind raced. They had been married for three months. From the first night, Aarav had always left her alone in their bedroom. She didn't know where he slept, she had always assumed it was the study because he worked late. But now, here he was, sitting on the bed, in the dead of night, shattering the quiet routine she had fallen into.

A sudden wave of self-consciousness washed over her. Had she been snoring? Did she look terrible with her hair all messed up from sleep? She wanted to ask, but the words seemed to catch in her throat, replaced by a strange kind of nervousness. But all the questions left her when she saw him shivering. Switching on the light, she turned towards him.

His face was pale, slick with sweat that plastered strands of dark hair to his forehead. His hands were clenched into fists, the knuckles white and strained. The silk duvet, usually tucked neatly around, lay in a tangled heap at the foot of the bed.

"Aarav?" Navya's voice was soft, laced with the lingering fog of sleep. She reached out her hand hesitantly, her fingers brushing tentatively against his damp arm. He flinched, a small, almost imperceptible jump, but didn't turn to her.

"Aarav, what's wrong?" Her voice gained a little more urgency, a tremor of concern creeping into its tone.

He finally turned, his eyes dark and wide, pupils dilated. For a brief moment, she saw terror cross his face before he seemed to force it down, replacing it with a strained calmness that didn't quite reach his eyes.

"Nothing," he rasped, his voice hoarse like he'd been screaming. "Just... a bad dream."

Navya sat up, pulling the duvet around her. *A Nightmare?* She wondered to herself. She looked at him again. He was practically drowning in perspiration, his chest heaving with each uneven breath.

"Aarav, you're shaking," she said gently, her hand now firmly on his arm, her thumb gently stroking the tense muscles. "Your heart is racing. That's not just a bad dream."

He looked down at his clenched hands as if seeing them for the first time before slowly uncurling them, the tension slowly fading from his fingers. He took a deep, shuddering breath, then another, trying to regain control.

"It's alright," she murmured, her voice a soothing balm. "Just breathe with me. In... and out." She demonstrated, taking deep, slow breaths, and after a moment, Aarav followed, his chest rising and falling in a steadier rhythm.

Finally, he turned his face towards her, the fear gradually receding, leaving behind a hollow weariness.

"I didn't mean to wake you," he whispered, his voice barely audible.

Navya's brow furrowed.

"Aarav, you didn't wake me. I just woke up," A pang of confusion hit her. Had he been doing this every night? She'd never seen him like this. Had he been sleeping here at all? She couldn't remember him slipping into bed beside her. Maybe he did, and she didn't realize. She was a deep sleeper.

She noticed the slight tremor in his hands, the faint circles under his eyes, the almost invisible tension that clung to his shoulders. It was as if he was always on edge, even in sleep.

"Are you okay?" she asked, her voice soft and searching. She hesitated, then asked the question that had been nagging at her. "Does this happen often?"

He avoided her gaze, looking instead at the hands he had finally managed to relax.

"Sometimes," he admitted, his voice low.

"Sometimes?" She repeated, her confusion deepening. "Aarav, I... I don't understand. I don't even hear you come to bed. Do you even sleep?"

He finally met her eyes, his eyes saying something she couldn't quite decipher.

"I... I come in after you fall asleep," he said as he shifted his gaze. "And I get up before you wake up. I didn't want you to see," He shifted uncomfortably. "It's nothing... just scary dreams."

"Aarav," she said softly, her fingers intertwining with his. "Dreams... they can be scary, they can be real. You don't have to go through it alone. Not anymore."

Suddenly, as if a dam had broken, he leaned forward, his hand gripping hers tightly.

"It...it was... I was back there. I was back in that place." He shut his eyes tightly for a moment, like he was physically trying to shut something out.

Navya gently rubbed his knuckles with her thumb, her heart aching for him. She didn't know what 'that place' was, but she felt the weight of it in his words, in the tremor of his hand.

A sudden wave of protectiveness washed over Navya. He had been lying here, alone in the dark, battling these silent demons while she slept peacefully beside him. It wasn't just a nightmare, she realised, it was something deeper, something that haunted him. And she, his wife, had been completely oblivious.

He didn't offer any more information, and she didn't push further. She knew he'd share when he was ready. Or maybe he wouldn't. But that didn't change the way her heart ached for him in that moment.

Aarav lay back down, turning his back on her, but Navya didn't drift back to sleep. She was acutely aware of his presence next to her. She couldn't help but wonder what those dreams were like, what terrible things lurked in the shadows of his mind.

Aarav, impeccably dressed in a charcoal grey suit, stood beside Navya. Her emerald green saree beautifully highlighted her deep brown eyes, complimented her. They were posing for the cover of 'Business Titans,' a magazine that was covering the city's latest power couple.

The photographer, a flamboyant man named Andy, was guiding them.

"Aarav, more relaxed. Think power, but with love, yes? Navya, tilt your head a little, the eyes should smolder...Perfect!"

Navya, ever the professional despite the turmoil she knew Aarav was putting her through, shifted her pose, her hand lightly brushing his arm as she did. A jolt, not unpleasant, ran through Aarav.

"Okay, let's do one where you're looking at each other," Andy instructed, his voice bouncing off the studio walls. "Connection is key! Let them see the spark, the passion!"

Aarav turned, meeting Navya's gaze. Her eyes, usually filled with quiet grace, held something he had never seen before - a blush. He saw her soul beneath the surface, not the pawn he had imagined. And for a breath-stealing second, he just saw her.

He allowed a small smile to curve his lips, a genuine one, not the practiced smirk he usually wore. Navya mirrored it, her smile lighting up her face.

"See? That's it!" Andy clapped his hands together, his voice echoing with enthusiasm. "You two are magic! Like a painting, a masterpiece! Lean in a bit, Aarav. Yes, yes! Perfect for the cover!"

Aarav instinctively tilted his head closer to hers, her warmth radiating towards him. A lock of her hair escaped her elaborate updo and fell across her cheek. Without thinking, he gently tucked it behind her ear, his fingers brushing against her soft skin. The contact felt electric. It was a small gesture, almost unconscious, but it spoke volumes.

Navya's breath hitched. She could see the confusion, the hopeful longing in his eyes, and for a heart-stopping moment, she wanted to forget everything that he had done to hurt her. Forget everything and just... pull him into her arms.

And Aarav, he was lost in those eyes. Eyes that now carried only affection for him. He could see the way she looked at him now, the way she admired him. He knew she was getting drawn towards him despite him hurting her so much. He wished she was as innocent as she was showing herself to be. He wished she had revealed everything to her before marriage. He wished...

"Lovely! That's beautiful!" Andy cooed, his camera clicking away relentlessly, capturing the tender exchange.

And then, like a slap in the face, it returned. The sharp, stinging reality of Aarav's situation. He wasn't supposed to take care of Navya or admire her. He hated her!

The smile vanished. His jaw clenched, and the warmth he had felt only moments ago was replaced by an icy chill. He stepped back abruptly, creating distance between them, his eyes turning hard. The casual affection was replaced by a cold mask of controlled indifference.

"Okay, that's enough," he said, his voice clipped, his focus on the photographer, "I think we have what we need."

Navya's smile faltered, her eyes, which had been so bright just moments ago, clouded over with hurt and confusion. The shift in him was jarring, like a sudden gust of icy wind. She swallowed, trying to maintain her composure.

"Yes, I suppose we do," she said, her voice barely a whisper, the warmth he'd briefly seen, frozen over.

Andy, oblivious to the tension, was still buzzing with excitement.

"Magnificent! We have the cover! Now the individual shots!"

Aarav turned away, his back rigid, ignoring Navya's questioning gaze. The lie was back in place, as firmly as ever. He was someone who wanted vengeance, he reminded himself, not the man who almost touched her cheek with tenderness. He refused to allow himself to succumb to the treacherous pull of her genuine, loving nature. Not once. Not ever.

♡♡♡

TWENTY-ONE

BLAST FROM THE PAST

The aroma of food filled the Singhania household. Aarav, leaning against the kitchen counter, checked his watch for the fifth time in as many minutes. The clock on the wall seemed to mock his impatience, ticking a little too slowly. He glanced at the dining table, neatly set, but with empty chairs.

"You keep staring at the door like you expect her to materialize out of thin air, bhai," Aryan teased, smirking as he watched TV in the living room.

Aarav rolled his eyes.

"You brat! Go and have dinner! It's getting late. You too, Avni."

Avni looked up at him, shifting her attention from her book to her brother.

"Let Bhabhi come, we should wait for her."

"You can eat if you are hungry," Aryan added.

Just as Aarav was about to reply, the front door clicked open, and Navya appeared. She looked tired, her hair slightly disheveled, but her eyes sparkled when she saw them. A genuine, warm smile spread across her face, making the exhaustion seem less pronounced. Both Aryan and Avni's faces lit up, their little frowns of worry dissolving into pure joy.

"Bhabhi!" Avni exclaimed, throwing her book aside and rushing to hug her. Aryan switched off the TV and went towards the kitchen.

Aarav felt a rush of fondness engulf him. They were all so happy to see her, a testament to the warmth Navya brought with her.

"Sorry I'm late," Navya said, brushing a few stray strands of her hair behind her ear. "The last-minute rush at the boutique... it's always crazy."

"No worries, Bhabhi," Aryan said as he offered her water. "We were just keeping Bhai company while he worried about you."

Navya's eyes flickered to Aarav. He didn't react. She knew Aarav wasn't worried. Yet, a warmth bloomed in her chest at Aryan's teasing. A silly and almost childish feeling. She knew it wasn't true, probably just Aryan's usual naughtiness, but the idea that Aarav might have been even the slightest bit concerned about her brought a delicate rush of pleasure. It was a whisper of something she knew was unlikely, but still, it made the exhaustion of the day seem just a little lighter.

"I was worried for you two," Aarav said in a defensive tone. "It's past dinner time and everyone is waiting for her."

"You are included in 'everyone', Bhai," Avni said, rolling her eyes.

"Just give me two minutes. Then we'll eat together," Navya said and rushed towards her room.

"You never offered me water when I come home tired," she heard Aarav say and chuckled.

Soon, they were all seated around the table, the earlier quiet replaced by a lively atmosphere of conversation. Navya shared anecdotes about her day at the boutique, her passion evident in every word, while Aryan and Avni filled her in on their day. Aarav just listened. He watched as Navya effortlessly engaged with his siblings, their laughter mingling with the clinking of cutlery. This was a feeling that made his heart fill with contentment.

Midway through dinner, Aarav cleared his throat.

"Navya, I have something to tell you."

She turned her gaze.

"Yes?"

"There's a...well, my college reunion party," he said, a touch of nervousness creeping into his voice. "We were invited. Would you like to join me?"

"Of course," she answered.

The easy acceptance brought a wave of relief. He had been half-expecting her to decline politely or show some hesitation. Or think of it as another PR stunt. He was glad she agreed.

Navya lay on the bed, her eyes closed but not actually sleeping. She was waiting for Aarav, who always came late at night when he thought she was asleep.

A while later she felt him slip under the duvet and soon enough, he was snoring lightly.

Hearing him snore, Navya shifted closer. Her movements were slow and deliberate so as not to startle him. She slipped her arm beneath his back, the cool skin of her forearm making gentle contact with his. He didn't stir. She slid closer until she could feel the heat radiating from his body, the restless shift of his shoulder against hers. Then, very slowly, she slid her other arm across his chest, resting her hand gently on his heart. It was beating fast, a frantic drum against her palm.

This was a private act, a silent promise to protect him from the shadows that haunted his sleep. She held him close as if he was a fragile piece of art she had to guard, his head nestled against her shoulder. She stayed like that, her body a warm anchor against his fear.

Earlier, he had been suffering alone in the dark while she slept peacefully beside him. Since the day she had known this, she had been followed by a surge of protective love.

Yes, she was in love. The girl who had sworn off love after it had ripped her heart out, was now drowning in it. With the man who hadn't been kind to her since their marriage, who hadn't been gentle in the slightest way.

Navya wanted to laugh hysterically at the absurdity of it all. She, the girl who had vowed never to fall in love again, was head over heels in love. She was in love, madly, deeply, intensely, passionately, with her husband, who hated her.

He hated her for some reason, a reason she was oblivious to. The reason that she needed to find out. She just hoped that whatever it was, it was something she could fix, something that was fixable. The thought of him hating her forever was something she couldn't even imagine now.

She closed her eyes, allowing herself to sleep.

Aarav blinked, focusing on the ceiling. He usually woke with a knot of dread, his heart hammering a chaotic rhythm against his ribs. It had been the same for years - ever since his parents had passed away; the nightmares, vivid and terrifying, a nightly reminder of a loss. But this morning... nothing.

He glanced down. Navya was nestled against his side, her arm draped firmly across his torso, her head nestled in the crook of his shoulder. He could feel the soft rise and fall of her breath against his skin. It was the grip of a child seeking comfort, a gesture so innocent it sent a strange current through him.

He carefully shifted, trying to extract himself without disturbing her, but her hold tightened.

"Aarav," she mumbled, her voice still thick with sleep. The sound, so close, so intimate, made his chest constrict. He hadn't realized how used he had become to silence in this room. He had deliberately kept himself emotionally detached, building walls around himself so high that even his voice seemed to echo within their confines.

"Just... getting up," he replied, his voice a low rumble that surprised even him.

She stirred again, nuzzling her face deeper into his shoulder. He could feel her soft hair tickling his neck. For a moment, he was still, his breath caught in his chest.

A small, involuntary smile tugged at the corner of his lips. He couldn't deny that Navya was a baby when she slept.

"Hmm," Navya murmured, her fingers clutching at the fabric of his shirt. "Few more minutes."

He froze. He wasn't used to being held, to being wanted like this. It was disorienting and strangely comforting. But he knew she was still in deep sleep.

"Navya, I have to get ready," he tried to sound firm, but his voice lacked its usual edge.

"You always get ready and leave before I wake up," she murmured and held him more tightly.

He sighed and slipped out from the bed.

As he moved towards the bathroom, Aarav couldn't shake the feeling that something had shifted in the room, in his life. He had woken up without a nightmare, wrapped in Navya's arms. And for the first time since his parent's death, that morning sun didn't feel quite so cold. He was still unsure what was happening, but a tiny seed of something new, something he couldn't ignore, had been planted.

Avni's eyes furrowed in concentration, trying to recreate her Bhabhi's famous chai. Aarav leaned against the kitchen counter, arms crossed, watching his younger sister with a barely concealed smirk. Aryan, perched precariously on a stool, was offering unsolicited advice on the spice ratio, which Avni promptly ignored. Navya, meanwhile, was meticulously arranging a plate of cookies she'd baked earlier, a soft smile playing on her lips.

It was a holiday and as promised, Navya was teaching Avni to make Chai, while the brothers waited to appreciate their little sister's considerable efforts.

“Bhabhi, these look amazing!” Aryan exclaimed; his eyes wide with admiration as he plucked a cookie. “Can I have another?”

“Of course, Aryan,” Navya chuckled, her gaze flicking towards Aarav for a millisecond, then quickly retreating.

Avni, finally satisfied with her chai, poured it into mismatched mugs.

"Okay, taste now! Everyone, be honest.

They each took a sip, their faces reflecting various states of approval. Avni watched them, bouncing on the balls of her feet with anticipatory energy.

"It’s really good, Kiddo," Aryan said around a mouthful of cookie.

Avni smiled. Then her gaze settled on Aarav.

"What about you, Bhai?"

Aarav took another sip, his expression unreadable. He saw the expectant look in Avni’s eyes, and more surprisingly, the quiet hope in Navya’s gaze.

"It’s...good," he muttered, his voice gruff. "Almost as good as Navya’s. Although I love Navya’s more, this is also fine.”

Avni beamed with happiness. Aarav smiled seeing the happiness of his sister.

“You like the tea I make??” Navya asked.

Aarav looked at her, momentarily caught off guard. Her eyes, dark and earnest, met his. Since marriage, he had criticized every effort made by her, including cooking. Lately, he had started getting used to the tea made by her.

“Of course, Bhabhi,” Aryan rolled his eyes. You make the best chai! Just like Bhai prefers.”

Aryan straightened up, his features hardening into a familiar mask of cold indifference.

“Don’t be ridiculous, Aryan,” Aarav said, setting the mug down with a clatter, the sound echoing suddenly. He deliberately avoided looking at Navya, his gaze fixed on some distant point beyond the window. "I am not particularly fond of over-spiced chai."

He turned and walked out of the kitchen, leaving behind a tableau of confused siblings and Navya, who could feel the sting of his words, her hope momentarily shattered into a million pieces. The accidental appreciation, and the moment’s fleeting truth, felt like a distant dream. And yet, somewhere, buried deep beneath the surface, a tiny spark of something lingered, refusing to be fully extinguished.

The thrum of bass vibrated through Aarav's chest as he and Navya stepped into the brightly lit party hall. It was a kaleidoscope of familiar faces, a nostalgic montage of his college days. He plastered a smile on his face, the kind that didn't quite reach his eyes, and offered Navya his arm. She looped her fingers through his, her grip a little too tight for his comfort.

He hated how her hand felt in his – soft, yielding, and perfect. He hated the way she supported him, the way she looked at him, and cared for him and his siblings. He had told her multiple times that he would never accept her as his wife, but he had also come to terms with the bitter truth - Navya hadn't just accepted him, she was starting to fall for him. She never told him, but there were a million instances that were hints. He would only be a fool to not realise it.

Aarav scanned through the room, to find old friends when across the crowd, his eyes met hers.

Samaira.

TWENTY-TWO

THE REUNION PARTY

Samaira.

The room seemed to blur around Aarav.

A wave of emotions crashed through him - surprise, confusion, and a raw, painful longing. It had been years, years of silence, years of pretending she didn't exist, years spent trying to forget the intoxicating pull she held over him. And here she was, as radiant as the day he had first fallen for her.

Navya squeezed his arm.

"Aarav? Is everything alright?"

"Yeah, just... catching up with the faces, you know."

She didn't believe him. She had followed his gaze.

"Samaira?" Navya asked and Aarav nodded.

Aarav had told her about Smaira before their marriage. He has wanted everything to be transparent between them, if only she had done the same...

They heard an announcement. Raghav, one of Aarav's classmates, was holding a microphone and speaking into it exuberantly.

"I am so glad you all made it today, with your significant other. I hope you all enjoy meeting old friends and greeting new people. Let the party begin!"

"Wait," Aarav saw Roshni, another friend climb the stage. "I want to confess something before we get to partying. It's been a weight on my heart for years. May I?"

"Sure," Raghav said as he offered her the microphone.

"Nayan," Roshni took a deep breath. "I want to confess something to you."

Nayan's eyes widened and everyone started shouting excitedly.

"You remember in your second year when you were suspended for a week because you mixed the wrong chemicals in the chemistry lab in class 12th and some equipment got burnt?"

"Yeah...?" he frowned.

"It wasn't you. It was me who did that. I am so sorry you were punished."

The whole room went silent and Nayan fumed in anger.

"I was grounded for a month!"

Roshni just looked at him apologetically. After a while, everyone burst out laughing including Nayan and Roshni.

"It's okay," Nayan said as he shook his head.

"This is fun," Raghav chipped. "Let's have a secret revealing session!"

The crowd cheered at the announcement. One by one, everyone revealed their secrets, like cheating in exams, bullying a junior, having a crush on a teacher, etc.

"Aarav," Nayan giggled, "who was the one you actually pined for back then? Come on, spill!"

A hush fell over the little group gathered, and Aarav tried to laugh it off, even though his face was pale.

"I am with my wife tonight, guys. Let it be."

"Samaira!" someone blurted out.

Aarav's heart skipped a beat and he turned to see his old best friend Varun smiling at him.

"You were utterly head over heels for Samaira, buddy! Everyone knew it except her, I guess!"

The room stilled and there was an eerie silence.

Aarav's hand, which rested lightly against the small of Navya's back, stiffened. He turned to her, his eyes a stormy grey, a mixture of guilt and something she couldn't quite decipher.

"Navya, I..."

But the words seemed to catch in his throat. He glanced back at the group, who were now staring at them with a morbid curiosity.

"It's fine, Aarav," Navya said, smiling at him. "We all had crushes in college. It's fine."

The crowd clapped. Aarav smiled back at her and his gaze then fell on Samaira. She was looking at him intently, way too intently. Uncomfortable, he pulled his gaze away from her.

Soon, the attention shifted to someone else and Aarav sighed in relief.

"Why is she coming towards us?" he heard Navya say and looked up at her.

Navya was looking ahead, her brows furrowed. Aarav followed her gaze and saw Samaira walking towards them.

"Hey, Aarav. How are you?" Samaira's voice was gentle. Aarav felt Navya's grip tightened on his arm.

"Hey Samaira," Aarav replied. "It's good to see you." He then turned, slightly, towards Navya. "This is my wife, Navya."

"Hello," she gently smiled. "You have a beautiful wife, Aarav."

Navya returned the smile, though it felt stiff and uncomfortable.

"It's nice to meet you, Samaira."

Aarav's hand tightened almost imperceptibly around Navya's.

"How have you been, Sam?"

The conversation felt stilted, the unspoken history between Aarav and Samaira made Navya uneasy. Samaira leaned closer to Aarav, her voice dropping to a conspiratorial level.

"So, how's married life treating you? Arranged marriages can be...interesting, can't they? It's such a different approach than, say, choosing someone you know you genuinely connect with," She directed a pointed glance at Navya, a subtle challenge in her eyes.

Navya's jaw tightened. She knew it was a veiled jab, a hint that she wasn't good enough for Aarav. She wanted to retort, to defend herself, but she knew that sinking to that level was exactly what Samaira wanted.

"I think the connection is pretty strong," he said, his voice sharper than it had been all night. He turned to Navya, whose eyes were wide with surprise at his words. "Don't they say arranged marriages are actually made in heaven, Navya? "

Navya didn't miss a beat. She laced her fingers through Aarav's, holding his hand tight. She moved closer to Aarav,and tucked her hand possessively under his arm, squeezing it. A wave of boldness washed over her.

"Absolutely," she said, her eyes flitting from Aarav to Samaira, a knowing smile on her lips. "And, I am sure you use social media."

Samaira's smile faltered for a split second.

"Oh, that's.. that's great," she faked a smile.

Suddenly, a voice cut through the air.

"Samaira! Fancy seeing you here," Megha, strode towards them with a flute of champagne in her hand.

Blood drained out Samaira's face.

"Megha! How lovely to see you too." She tried to sound casual, but Navya noticed a flash of discomfort in her eyes.

Megha took a generous sip of her champagne.

"So, Samaira, how's... how's everything going? Still enjoying the soon to be single life, I presume?" Megha's voice was deceptively sweet.

"What?" Aarav asked in confusion.

Samaira laughed, a brittle sound.

"Yes, very much so. Some things just aren't meant to be, you know? Better to move on than to be stuck in something that doesn't work."

Megha's eyebrow arched, and she let out a small, knowing chuckle.

"Oh, I agree, completely. Especially when the 'something' stops being financially viable, right? Like when the person you promised to stay with 'in sickness and in health' loses their job, and suddenly the whole 'forever' thing becomes rather tedious?" She paused, making eye contact with Samaira, her smile widening ever so slightly. "Right, Samaira? Isn't that how it is with your husband? You filed for divorce because he lost his job, right?"

A hush fell over their small circle. Samaira's face turned an unflattering shade of red, the poised facade crumbling. The air crackled with the revelation. Navya's eyes widened in surprise as she looked at Samaira.

"Megha!" Aarav said sharply, a warning in his tone.

Megha just shrugged, seemingly unfazed.

"Just keeping it real, Aarav. Besides, someone had to stop this nonsense," she turned to Navya and squeezed her shoulder. "Navya, sorry I am late, you must have listened to her crap."

Samaira glared at Megha before turning on her heel and walking away, the red of her gown seeming to fade into the mass of people.

"You are always on time, sweetheart!" Navya said as she hugged Megha.

The sting of Samaira's words was still there, but Navya was happy that Aarav had taken a stand for her. Also, Megha's bluntness had shut Samaira's mouth. Strangely, it had made Navya feel a little bit stronger, a little more sure of her place beside Aarav, despite their complicated pasts, and their far more complicated present.

TWENTY-THREE

BEYOND THE SHADOWS

Navya sat on the bed, her fingers tracing the delicate floral pattern on the duvet cover. Aarav was in the bathroom, she could hear the water flowing. She thought things were improving between them but Aarav had returned to his shell. A cold, distant creature inhabiting the same space as her.

She had tried, tried so hard, to connect. To get past the icy shell he had built around himself. She had cooked his favorite meal and had tried to initiate a light conversation about their families. All met with the same dismissive silence, the same subtle glare that sent shivers down her spine, not of excitement, but of unease.

The bathroom door clicked open, and Aarav emerged, his hair still damp, droplets clinging stubbornly to his eyelashes. He looked at her for a moment, she usually slept longer. Walking past her without a word, he headed straight for the closet.

"Aarav?" Navya's voice was barely a whisper, but it held a fragile hope. He paused, his back still to her.

"Hmm?" His tone was flat, devoid of any warmth.

"Can we...can we talk?" she asked, her hands twisting in her lap.

He sighed, a sound of pure annoyance.

"About what? If it's not important, I am getting late for office," he pulled out a crisp white shirt, his movements quick and precise, as if he wanted the interaction over as soon as possible.

"It's important," she pressed, the word catching in her throat. "It's about us."

He finally turned to face her, and for a fleeting moment, she caught a glimpse of something in his eyes – not anger, not disdain, but pain. It was gone in a heartbeat, replaced by that familiar wall.

"There's nothing to talk about us," he said, his voice clipped. He began to button his shirt, avoiding her gaze.

"Is it because Samaira is back?" She couldn't stop the tears from welling in her eyes, frustration and hurt rising in her chest like a tide.

He stopped buttoning his shirt, finally meeting her eyes.

"Are you out of your mind?" His voice was sharper now, edged with a dangerous impatience. "Don't ever say that again."

"Then just tell me, what have I done!" she retorted, her voice rising. "I am fed up, Aarav! You can't keep hurting my emotions like this all the time! I am doing everything you tell me to. What else do you want from me?"

"I just need some peace! Let me breathe, that's it!" Aarav said, his voice tight, almost breaking.

He turned away again, resuming his routine. Navya watched him, her heart pounding with a confusing mix of emotions. He was deflecting, avoiding her direct questions. It felt so deliberate, so practiced. It wasn't just coldness; it was something he was trying to hide. A secret, perhaps. She remembered the fleeting glimpse of pain she had seen in his eyes. It wasn't directed at her; it was his own turmoil.

Aarav finished getting ready, ignored her, and left the room.

The afternoon sun bled through the gaps in the blinds, casting striped shadows across Aarav's office. He sat on the table, staring at his computer, not working, just looking at it.

A sharp knock startled him. He knew that it would be Megha. She'd been doing this more often lately - dropping by every two days.

"Hey," she said, her voice a little too cheerful for the circumstances. "How was the meeting?"

Aarav forced a weak smile.

"As usual."

Megha didn't buy it. She could read him like a book, even when he tried to slam the cover shut. She walked over and perched on the table, her eyes direct and unwavering.

"Aarav," she began, her voice softening, "We need to talk."

He sighed, running a hand through his hair. He'd been avoiding this. He'd been avoiding everything, honestly.

"About what?" he asked, feigning ignorance.

"Don't play dumb with me, Aarav. You've been... off. For months now. And it's not just a bad mood. There's something else, something serious." She paused, letting her words sink in. "It's about Navya, isn't it?"

Aarav's jaw tightened. He looked away, focusing on the pattern on the monitor.

"What makes you say that?" His voice was strained, betraying his carefully constructed nonchalance.

Megha leaned forward, her hands clasped together in her lap.

"It's obvious, Aarav. The way you flinch when her name is mentioned. The forced smiles around her. You barely make eye contact with anyone anymore." she paused. "I talked to Navya."

His head snapped up, shocked.

"She told me that it's like you're living in the same house, but worlds apart. And also that, you told her you would make her life hell."

He remained silent, the tension building. The truth was a coiled serpent in his chest, threatening to strike. He wanted to deny it, to tell Megha that she was imagining things, but the lie felt too heavy.

"We're just... going through a rough patch," he finally managed, the words sounding brittle even to his ears.

Megha shook her head, her gaze filled with concern and frustration.

"Aarav, 'rough patch' doesn't explain this. You're miserable, and I know you're not someone who hides things easily. You used to talk to me about everything - even about the time you had accidentally glued your hand to a poster in kindergarten! So, what is it? What's really going on with Navya?"

He could feel the walls collapsing around him. He knew he should tell her, she deserved to know. He hated the secrecy, the way it was eating him from the inside out. But the words, the specific, horrible truths, were like barbed wire caught in his throat.

He looked at Megha, her face a mirror of his own pain. He saw the worry in her eyes, the deep love she held for him. He wanted to confide in her, to finally unload the burden he had been carrying. But something, an internal force, held him back.

"It... it hurts Megha," he whispered, the admission barely audible.

"Aarav, you need to talk to someone. You can't keep this bottled up forever. This is destroying you, I can see it."

He stared at his hands, the silence filling the room once more. He knew she was right. He knew he was slowly drowning in his own silence. But the reasons, the roots of his hatred for Navya, were too painful to speak aloud.

"I... I just can't," he said, finally, his voice barely a whisper. He looked at Megha, his eyes pleading for understanding that he couldn't explain. "Maybe... maybe someday. But not now."

Megha's gaze softened. She knew she couldn't force him. Not now. She reached out and gently placed her hand over his.

"Okay," she said, her voice full of compassion. "But promise me you'll think about it. And promise me you won't let this consume you."

Aarav nodded, unable to meet her eyes. He knew he was making a promise he couldn't keep. The unspoken walls between the truth and the world, between him and Navya, were still standing tall, and he was still trapped as the walls suffocated him.

The first sliver of light, a pale intruder through the curtains, nudged Aarav awake. His mind, as always, felt foggy at first, like a half-forgotten dream clinging to the edges of his consciousness. He blinked and his eyes caught Navya's face. His hand surrounded her waist and his hands were holding her protectively.

He carefully sat up, not disturbing her sleep. Reaching for his phone on the nightstand, he quickly checked the time, a habit.

6:30 AM. Another full night's uninterrupted sleep.

He shifted on the mattress.

It was strange. The nightmares, the ones that used to claw their way into his sleep, had been absent for months. He tried to recall the last time he had woken up in a panic. He couldn't. It was a blank, a gaping hole in his memory where all the terror had been. He had been so used to waking up in a cold sweat, heart hammering, that he would count the days he had nightmares. Days which had become months now.

He usually woke up with this feeling. The feeling that he had held her tight, perhaps even whimpered in his sleep. He would be filled with a strange guilt. Navya had never complained.

He looked at her sleeping form again. He had a faint memory of a gentle weight against his side, the soft curve of a body curved in his, and pulling him into arms. He quickly shook his head, berating himself. He was the one who had night terrors, not her. She was not the one who needed comfort. He must have held her again.

He sighed quietly, a soft sound that didn't disturb the silence of the room. He slid out of bed, his feet landing softly on the rug. He needed to get some coffee. Today, like every morning, the lingering mystery would gnaw at him. Why were his nights so peaceful now? What helped him sleep so profoundly? It was a question he knew would keep him guessing until he finally found the answer.

TWENTY-FOUR
THE UNVEILING

Navya closed her laptop and sighed. The Zoom meeting finally ended after running for hours. She was on her way to the office when a client called for a zoom meeting in 10 minutes. Luckily, she was passing by this restaurant. She looked at her watch and it was almost lunchtime.

She convinced herself that a solo lunch would be empowering, a mini act of rebellion against the stifling routine her life had become. The restaurant was bright and bustling, unlike the muted silence that permeated her home in the absence of Aryan and Avni. But the vibrant atmosphere was instantly muted by the scene in front of her.

There, by the window, bathed in the afternoon sun, sat Aarav. Not the Aarav she knew, the man with the perpetual furrow between his brows, the man who barely made eye contact. This Aarav was relaxed, his face animated, and a genuine smile played on his lips. And right opposite him, she sat, her hand resting lightly on his wrist. Samaira

Navya felt the breath catch in her chest, a sharp, painful sting. Samaira's laughter was light and melodic and washed over Navya as if mocking the silence that she and Aarav shared.

She watched them, frozen in place, feeling a strange detachment. It was like watching a scene from someone else's life, a tragic movie unfolding before her eyes. The food she had ordered sat untouched on the table. Trying to control the pang in her heart, she paid the bill and walked towards her car.

It had been an hour, but Aarav hadn't come back home yet. The images flashed continuously in her mind - Aarav, laughing, his head thrown back, his eyes shining at Samaira. The sight had twisted something tight and painful inside her. It was one thing to feel a growing distance between her and Aarav, to sense the coldness that had become a constant presence; it was another to see him so openly happy with someone else.

Aarav entered and walked past her without acknowledging her.

"You were with her," Navya said, her voice raspy, trembling despite her attempts to sound composed. "You were with her, Aarav. Don't you dare lie to me!"

Aarav stopped with his back to her. He didn't turn or flinch. It was as if her words had no more impact than a gentle breeze. She blinked as she watched him ignore her while unbuckling his watch. His silence was like a slap, confirming everything she feared.

"I saw you. You were laughing. You looked... happy," Tears pricked at the corners of her eyes, but she refused to let them fall. Not yet. Not in front of him. "Is this what you always dreamt of, Aarav? Is it finally happening? Are you with her? Is that it? Is that why you've been so distant?"

Finally, he turned. His face was a mask of controlled fury, his jaw clenched tight. An affair. That was her go-to explanation, the easiest way for her to reconcile his coldness. The accusation stung because it was so utterly, frustratingly wrong.

"Distant?" he repeated, his voice dangerously low. "That's what you think this is about? Some stupid affair?" He walked towards her, each step a heavy thud against the hardwood.

Navya recoiled in fear. The coldness she had felt from him these past few months wasn't just indifference; it was deeper and darker, and she had sensed it. The simmering anger, the barely-contained resentment, but she had never understood its root.

"Tell me!" she demanded, her voice cracking. "Tell me why! Why do you barely look at me? Why do you come to the bedroom after I fall asleep and leave before I wake up? Why do you act like I am nothing to you? You accept it or not, but I am your wife, Aarav. Not a ghost in your house. You treat me like I am invisible and like I am some disease you can't shake off!" She crossed her arms, trying to project an illusion of strength. Underneath, she felt a gaping hole opening up inside her. "Why do you hate me when *I love you so much!"*

It was a confession that seemed both utterly absurd and heartbreakingly true. A confession that, but somehow, made Aarav's pain even sharper.

He didn't know what to believe. Was this a desperate attempt to manipulate him? A genuine confession? Or something in between? For the first time, he saw not the woman who he hated but the woman who truly loved him.

"I love you, Aarav," Navya choked out, tears tracking paths through the streaks on her face. "I love you so much that it hurts. I don't even know why you hate me so much?"

She finally confessed. She couldn't take it anymore. The idea that he loathed her was painful but the thought of him with another woman was worse.

He stepped closer, each movement deliberate, each footfall a heavy drumbeat of impending revelation.

"Hate you? Navya, hate doesn't even begin to cover it. My hatred for you is a living thing, a burning inferno that consumes me." He paused, his breath coming in ragged gasps. He could feel the long-buried pain, the gnawing ache in his chest, rising to the surface.

"For months, I have kept it to myself. I have borne it, tried to understand, to find some reason to... to tolerate your presence. But you want to know?"

A muscle twitched in his jaw. He closed the distance between them, his eyes boring into her, and a storm brewing in them.

"You want to know why, Navya? Do you really want to know why I can't stand being around you? Why do I hate you?"

Navya's breath hitched. The sheer intensity of his hatred made her stagger back. She had expected anger, maybe denial, but not this raw loathing.

"I... I don't understand..." Her voice was barely a whisper.

He laughed. A harsh, brittle sound scraped against her ears.

"You wouldn't. You wouldn't understand the pain, the absolute hell you've put me through, the reason why I've been living a goddamn lie for months. And you dare accuse me of an affair. When you... when you killedthem."

Navya's brow furrowed, confusion warring with the terror gripping her.

"Killed... who? What are you talking about?"

"My parents," he spat out, the words like acid on his tongue. He grabbed her shoulders, his grip tight enough to bruise. "*You killed my parents*, Navya. You are the reason they are dead. Samaira didn't cause me this pain. You did. You are the sole reason I am in so much pain! Not because I am in love with Samaira. I was over her long ago. No, my pain is because I hate you, Navya, more than I thought was possible."

ASHES OF YESTERDAY, SPARKS OF TOMORROW

TWENTY-FIVE
LOVE AND LOATH

The file lay open on the bed. Navya stared at the words. It was all there: the police report, news articles, and a picture of her old car.

Not her car, technically. Almost two decades old, a hand-me-down from her father when he had upgraded. But the model, the year, the license plate – were all there. The car that had collided with the vehicle Aarav's parents had been driving. The car that had ended their lives.

Navya's world shattered. Her breath hitched in her throat as she processed the reason. She had killed his parents? It was a bizarre accusation. It felt so heavy that it threatened to crush her. She racked her brain, desperately trying to find even the sliver of logic in his claim. She barely knew his family. How could she have possibly been responsible for their deaths?

A cold dread began to bloom in her chest. This wasn't some petty squabble or a difference in opinion. This was a deep-seated, irrational hatred rooted in a tragedy she had absolutely no connection to.

Aarav sat on the edge of the bed, his back to her, his posture stiff and unforgiving. He hadn't spoken a word since he had revealed it all to her.

"Aarav," Navya's voice was barely a whisper, choked with fear and pleading. "Tell me...tell me this isn't true."

He didn't move.

"Aarav, please," she begged as she took a tentative step closer to him. "The article... It says my car was involved... your parents..." Her voice broke, the words trapped in her throat.

Finally, he turned, and the look on his face was worse than anything she could have imagined. It wasn't just anger, it was a cold, searing grief that had burrowed deep into his soul. His eyes, once warm and tender, looked like shards of ice.

"So you finally know," he said, his voice a low growl devoid of any other emotion but bitterness. "You finally understand why I can't stand the sight of you."

Navya recoiled as if struck.

"But... how... why didn't you ever tell me?"

"Tell you?" Aarav laughed, a harsh, humorless sound that sent shivers down her spine. "What would have changed, Navya? What would have changed if I told you? Would doing so have brought my parents back to life? Would it have erased the fact that your car, the one you were driving, killed them?"

Her breath hitched in her chest. The words hit her like a physical blow. She could feel her world crumbling around her, brick by agonizing brick.

"I-I don't understand. I don't remember..."

"Of course, you don't remember," Aarav said, standing up, his movements jerky and filled with suppressed rage. "You were drunk, Navya. You were so drunk that you couldn't remember the damage you caused that night. So drunk that you never realized you killed someone."

Each word of the accusation was a poisoned dart piercing Navya's heart. She stared at him, her mind reeling, trying to grasp the enormity of what he was saying. She didn't remember anything even close to an accident in her life.

"I... I was... ?" she stammered, the truth struggling against her shattered recollections. "I... I don't understand. Why did nothing ever come of this? Why was I never held accountable?"

"Money," Aarav spat out, the word a curse. "Your parents bought your way out of it, paid off the witness to shut his mouth. They silenced everyone. They buried the truth along with my parents. And they never even told me and duped me into marrying my parents' killer!"

Navya collapsed onto the bed, tears streaming down her face. The weight of Aarav's words, the brutal truth he had carried in silence for so long, was crushing her. She had unknowingly destroyed his family, and in turn, he had been living a lie with her every day.

"But that memory was a nightmare for me," Aarav's voice.broke

"I... I had no idea," she sobbed, her body wracked with guilt and despair. "I would never... if I had known..."

Aarav turned away, his face a mask of bitterness.

"It doesn't matter now, does it? All those blessings, the wishes, and the affection that your parents gave me were a mockery, weren't they? Every time they smiled at me, it was a painful reminder of what you took away."

He walked to the window, staring out at the city lights. The vibrant colors seemed dull and meaningless.

"Everything about you is a reminder of the life I lost."

He didn't look at her. He couldn't. The months of bottled-up anger and excruciating grief were finally exploding, and both of them were left standing in the wreckage. The veil was gone, the truth exposed. And now, both of them had to face the terrifying reality of what it meant for their marriage, for their lives.

The silence stretched between them, thick and suffocating. What had once been a promise of respect and partnership now felt like a noose tightening around their throats. The walls of their shared life began to close in, as both grappled with the implications of what this meant. Would their marriage crumble beneath the weight of grief and vengeance? Could they ever find a way to navigate the treacherous waters of their intertwined fates?

"But... why? Why marry me? If you knew... if you hated me so much..." Navya finally managed to say, a desperate grasp for logic in a world suddenly gone insane. "Why didn't you just hand me to the police?"

Aarav looked at her without reacting to her tears.

"After... After my parent's death, Aryan was barely sixteen, Avni just ten. They were lost, devastated. And then years later you... you came into their lives, a beacon of stability, a source of comfort."

He turned back to her, his gaze piercing.

"Aryan saw in you the warmth he craved, the guiding hand he desperately needed to navigate adulthood. Avni... she latched onto you like a drowning person to a lifeline. You became their anchor, and I couldn't snatch it away from them."

A sob escaped Navya's lips.

"They needed you, Navya," Aarav continued, his voice softening slightly, but the accusation remained sharp. "You were like a light in the darkness. And I... I couldn't take that away from them. Not even if it meant enduring a living hell."

He turned away; his silhouette outlined against the bright morning light.

"Every vow I took during the wedding, every smile that you flashed for me, every meal I shared with you, felt like a betrayal. A betrayal to my parents."

Navya stared at his rigid back, the weight of his words crushing her. The woman she thought she was, the life she thought she had, crumbled around her, leaving her standing in the ruins of a lie.

At that moment, the reality of their situation intensified. They were not just two people bound in an unwanted marriage; they were adversaries caught in a web of tragedy, forced to confront the ghosts of their pasts. The journey ahead loomed uncertain, fraught with pain.

TWENTY-SIX

THE BITTER TRUTH

Sunlight filtered weakly through the high windows of her office. Navya traced a finger across the brittle pages of a microfiche reader, her eyes scanning the digitized image of an old newspaper article. The headline screamed in bold, black ink:

"Tragic Accident Claims Lives of Couple Returning From Vacation. A blue Maruti Suzuki lost control on Highway 58, crashing into an oncoming SUV; Jagdish and Disha Singhania were pronounced dead at the scene while their son is recovering from minor injuries."

Her heart clenched. Even seeing it laid out like this, she couldn't accept the brutal truth.

She had spent the last few days in her office and the archives of the local police department, chasing any lead that could crack open the locked box of her memory. Each article, each police report, and each witness statement was a piece of a shattered mirror, reflecting fragments of a past she didn't recognize. The more she read, the more disoriented she felt. It was like trying to assemble a puzzle where half the pieces were missing, and the others were warped and faded.

Yes, she had a Maruti Suzuki, her father's old car that she had inherited years ago. It was the first car her Dad had bought for himself. But the information in the articles was stark, factual. There was nothing in the official reports that even hinted at what Aarav had suggested. There was no mention of her being at fault or reckless.

Yet, Aarav's unwavering certainty, the bitterness in his eyes, had planted a seed of doubt that was now a thorny plant pricking her. Had her parents really bribed the witness or the police? The idea that she might be responsible for Aarav's parents' deaths was like a poison seeping through her veins. She couldn't face Aarav, Aryan, and Avni so she avoided going home.

Navya leaned back in the hard chair, rubbing her temples. She was never so careless. She only drank occasionally, but never so much that she would not remember it. And she was sure, if she had drunk even a little, she would have never driven the car.

The digitized images of the wrecked SUV – the crumpled and twisted metal – swam before her eyes. It looked... violent. She tried to conjure up even a single, fleeting image from that night, a flash of memory, anything. But there was nothing. Only the same, suffocating blankness.

She closed the files, the image of the wrecked car still burned into her retinas. She needed more. She needed to talk to her parents about this.

Grabbing her bag, she left the office, the cold afternoon air stinging her face. She felt no closer to the truth, but she knew she couldn't give up. The weight of Aarav's accusations, and the gaping hole in her memory, all fueled her. She couldn't move on. She wouldn't until she understood what actually happened on that fateful night.

Rain lashed against the window panes of the Oberoi's living room, mirroring the storm brewing inside Navya. Her parents, Rajesh and Anjali sat stiffly on the plush sofa, their faces etched with a familiar, suffocating guilt.

"Just tell me if it's true," Navya pleaded, her voice barely a whisper. "Tell me what happened five years ago. Did I... Did an accident happen?" She swallowed the lump in her throat making it difficult to speak.

Anjali's eyes filled with tears, but she didn't speak. Rajesh cleared his throat as he wrapped his hand around his wife's.

"Dad, Mom, please," Navya fell to her knees. "I need to know."

"Navya, beta," Rajesh began, his voice strained, "some things are better left unsaid. It's... it's in the past."

"No!" Navya snapped. "It's not in the past! It's tearing me apart! It's tearing me and Aarav apart! Aarav says I don't remember it because I was drunk. But that doesn't explain why you're hiding it!"

The silence that followed was thick and heavy with unspoken accusations and buried secrets. The only sound was the relentless drumming of rain, a relentless rhythm hammering at the fragile peace of the room.

"Did I... did I really kill his parents, Dad?" Navya asked, her voice breaking. "And did you bribe people to silence them?

Rajesh's face paled and Anjali looked at her, horrified. Navya pressed on, her eyes fixed on their faces, desperate for answers.

"Five years," she whispered, more to herself than them. "For five years, Aarav has been living with nightmares."

Anjali let out a shaky breath.

"Navya, please," she pleaded, her voice laced with pain. "It's not... it's not as simple as it seems."

"Simple?" Navya laughed, a bitter, hollow sound. "Being branded a killer, having your marriage turned into a battlefield, unable to face your family. Of course, it's not simple, Mom."

Rajesh finally looked up, his eyes brimming with unshed tears.

"There were... complications. Things that... that would ruin lives if they came out."

"Yeah? What would have happened?" Navya demanded, her voice sharp. "My career would have finished? I hadn't even started, Dad. I would have ended up in jail? If I did something horrible then I deserved all that! But you didn't think even once about Aarav? The other two kids who lost their parents at such a young age?"

Rajesh looked at Anjali, a silent plea passing between them. The weight of their secret seemed to crush them. Then, Rajesh took a deep breath, the air catching in his throat.

"I did what I thought was best for my daughter," he confessed, his voice chcked with emotion. "I couldn't see her behind the bars even before her life started."

The confession was a bitter pill.

Anger simmered beneath the surface, a molten core threatening to erupt. Anger at her father, for his actions, for the lie that had sustained Aarav's life for five years, for stealing her right to face the truth, however painful.

The faces swam before her eyes: Aarav's, etched with a pain she hadn't understood until now; Aryan and Avni's faces, their smiles filled with respect and admiration. How could she face them now? How could she look Aarav in the eyes, knowing the devastation she had inadvertently caused?

Tears threatened to spill from her eyes, but Navya held them back, keeping a steel grip on her composure. The emotional turmoil was a cluster of confusion, guilt, and fear. Fear of losing Aarav whom she loved so much that she couldn't imagine a life without him now. Fear of seeing hatred in the eyes of Aryan and Avni, who had only admiration for her. The path ahead seemed impossibly long, dark, and uncertain.

TWENTY-SEVEN
THE RECKONING

Navya's heart pounded in her chest as she mustered the courage to enter her house, the weight of the revelation bearing down on her. The mere thought of facing Aryan and Avni filled her with a torrent of emotions – guilt, dread, and remorse, all intertwined in a web. She knew they loved her deeply, and she had grown to care for them like her own siblings. However, she was unsure how they would react when they discovered the truth about their parents' demise.

She had avoided this moment for days, but it was time for her to face Aryan, Avni, and Aarav.

Taking a deep breath, she pushed the door open. The thought of being home should have been comforting, but it only heightened the anxiety that gripped her. She stepped inside, each step feeling heavy, her heart pounding in her ears like a frantic drum.

"Bhabhi! You're back!" Aryan exclaimed, as soon as he saw her. "I missed you so much!"

"Bhabhi?" Avni ran out of her room, hearing Aryan.

She hugged Navya tightly.

"It's just not the same without you here. I am so glad you're home."

Navya felt a lump form in her throat.

"I've missed you both too," Navya admitted, her voice barely above a whisper.

Aryan and Avni led her into the living room, and sat across the sofa. They started talking about everything that they hadn't been able to tell her in these two days. She couldn't stop a tear that rolled from her eyes and quickly wiped it off.

Navya knew that Aryan and Avni would have their own feelings to grapple with once they learned of her involvement in their parents' deaths. She braced herself for their anger, pain, and their refusal to accept her. She could only imagine how difficult it would be for them to look at her the same way, knowing that she had been the cause of their unimaginable loss.

She worried that their bond would be irrevocably broken. After all, she had been a part of the family, someone they trusted and loved. But how could they continue to love her, knowing that she had robbed them of the very people who had given them life and love?

Navya wondered if they would ever be able to forgive her or if they would forever see her as the one who had taken their parents away.

The laughter, bright and sharp, cut through Aarav like shards of glass. He watched as Navya laughed at something Aryan had said. Laughing freely, unconcerned, nestled between her two siblings, as if nothing had ever happened.

His chest tightened, a suffocating pressure building with each playful jab from Aryan, each melodic giggle from Avni. They were a picture of familial bliss, a cruel mockery of the life Aarav had lost.

He walked towards them, his boots crunching on the gravel path, the sound a prelude to the storm brewing within him. Navya's laughter died in her throat as she saw him, the light in her eyes flickering and dying, replaced by a flicker of fear and pain. Aryan and Avni, sensing the shift in the atmosphere, fell silent, their faces etched with apprehension.

Aarav stopped directly in front of Navya, his gaze burning into her. The air crackled with unshed tears and simmering fury. He reached out, his hand gripping her arm with a force that made her wince, dragging her away from her siblings, their shocked expressions following them like accusing ghosts.

He hauled her into the relative darkness of the overgrown rose bushes bordering the property, thorns snagging at her clothes. He didn't care.

"Don't you have shame?" he snarled, his voice low and dangerously controlled. "You were laughing with them, pretending like...like nothing had happened. How could you, Navya?

Navya's eyes welled up, tears spilling down her cheeks. She tried to speak, to offer some explanation, but the words caught in her throat. The only sound was the ragged rasp of her breaths and the rustling of the rose bushes.

"I am sorry. So incredibly sorry."

Aarav's control snapped. All his composure crumbled under the weight of his fury and disbelief.

"Sorry?" he spat, the word tasting like ash in his mouth. "'Sorry' doesn't even begin to cover it. You are responsible for my parent's death, Navya! You made me and my siblings orphans! And you are saying sorry for taking my parents' lives?"

He took a shuddering breath, struggling to regain control of his voice. The words he spoke next tore at him as much as they wounded her. He wanted to hurt her, to make her feel even a fraction of the pain he was experiencing. It was a cruel, desperate attempt to ease his own agony.

"And then, you had the audacity, the sheer gall, to come to my siblings, to stand here in my house, pretending everything was normal?" His voice cracked the veneer of anger revealing the raw, bleeding wound beneath.

"Do you think it's easy for me, Aarav? Do you think I'm just waltzing through life? You don't realize what I am going through. I see Aryan and Avni destroyed every time I close my eyes. I am scared I am going to lose all this once they know the truth," her voice cracked with emotion. "It's not easy for me. This... this burden, it's crushing me from the inside out. Every breath I take feels like a betrayal."

She reached out a trembling hand as if to touch him, to plead for understanding. He flinched away.

"I know, Aarav. I know that I can never undo it. I can never make it right. But please," she whispered, her voice breaking completely. "Don't hate me. I know that I don't deserve your forgiveness, but please... don't hate me." Hot tears streamed down her face.

He saw the pain in her eyes, the genuine remorse, yet it did little to quell the tempest raging within him.

"Don't hate you?" he mocked, his voice laced with bitterness. "Don't hate you? I already hate you, Navya! More than you can imagine."

"You have every right to hate me. You should. But..." She took a deep, shuddering breath. "But I can't... I can't stop. I can't stop loving you. I love you, even though I know I don't deserve to."

TWENTY-EIGHT

Seeing Through the Hate

"I love you, even though I know that I don't deserve to."

Aarav didn't react to that.

"The accident... I don't remember it. I swear, I don't. If I had done it," she continued, her voice trembling, "I would have... I would have gone to the police. Faced it. I wouldn't have hidden. I swear I don't remember the accident, but what I always want to remember is that I love you."

Her pain was a physical presence, a tangible force that hung between them. It was the kind of pain that comes from a wound that has festered and been left untreated for far too long. Seeing it, hearing it, a strange shift began to occur within Aarav. The anger, the resentment he had nurtured for so long had begun to recede, replaced by a foreign sensation. It was not forgiveness, not yet.

It was a tug, he realized, deep in his chest. A compassion he hadn't known he was capable of, bloomed like a fragile flower pushing through cracked concrete. He looked at her, truly seeing her for the first time - not through the lens of his hurt, but as a person stripped bare by her own suffering. The implication of her words sank in. Had he been so blinded by his pain that he had overlooked the possibility of her innocence? Had he unfairly judged her?

No, this was the woman who took his parents away from him. This was the woman who made his siblings suffer. *But she also took care of them and was now their family.*

He turned and took a slow step towards her.

"Love?" he finally rasped, his voice rough. Each syllable felt like sandpaper scraping against his throat. "You speak of love to me, Navya? After everything?"

Navya flinched.

"I know," she whispered, her voice cracking. "I know you will never love me back. But I had to tell you."

"Do you think that confessing your love will erase the past? Will it bring my parents back?" His voice was laced with venom.

Her shoulders slumped, her gaze dropping to the floor.

"No, Aarav. Nothing can bring them back. I know that. But... I wanted you to know that I am not playing some game, this is not any twisted way to make things up. I..." she paused, taking a ragged breath, "I just wanted you to know that I love you."

It left him momentarily speechless. But the months of bitterness were a strong force, a deep wound that refused to heal.

"And what do you expect me to do with this information, Navya?" he asked, his voice dangerously low. "Applaud you? Thank you for taking my parents away and then telling me you love me?"

"I don't expect anything," she said quietly. "Not your love, not your forgiveness. But maybe now, this won't be a secret anymore. This... pain that has been between us for so long. Maybe this can give me the courage to fight for my love. I just want this pain to go away a little bit."

He wanted to lash out, to tell her that the past was irreparable, that they were forever bound by tragedy. But another part of him, buried deep inside, wondered if the pain could actually be lessened a little.

He closed his eyes, letting out a long, shaky breath.

"Maybe," he murmured, the word barely audible.

He opened his eyes, his gaze meeting hers. He could not give her the answer she expected. Nor could he deny her the truth.

"But this does not absolve your mistake," he added, his eyes blazing. "You can speak of this so-called love of yours. But for all these years, I have lived in hell. You can't expect me to wake up one morning and tell you that I forgive you."

"I... I understand," she whispered, the words catching in her throat. "I won't... I won't demand anything from you, Aarav. Not reciprocation of my love. Not even acknowledgment of my existence.

Tears blurred her vision, but she forced herself to hold his gaze. Even through the burning ache, she needed him to see her sincerity.

"My... my love for you isn't something I can control. It's... it's there, Aarav. It's a part of me now, like the air I breathe," she took a shaky step towards him. "I won't expect you to love me back. I'll never force you to. But... but please, don't ask me to stop. Don't ask me to deny the only good thing that has ever come out of this... this mess."

Shame burned through her, but the need to make him understand was stronger.

"Please, just... don't deny me the right to feel this," she pleaded, her voice hoarse. "Don't deny me the right to love you... even if it's one-sided, even if it hurts like hell"

Her voice finally crumbled, the question hanging in the air like a fragile butterfly caught in a storm.

Aarav stood there, his face a mask of conflicting emotions. She saw the pain evolving on his features, the confusion swirling in his dark eyes. But beneath that, she also caught a glimpse of something she couldn't quite decipher. Perhaps a sliver of... pity? Maybe even... a hint of a reluctant acknowledgment?

But he didn't speak. He didn't offer any words of comfort, any sign of understanding, or even a further rejection. He simply stared at her, his chest rising and falling in uneven breaths as if he were caught in an internal battle.

He hated her. He should hate her. He had to hate her. It was the foundation upon which his existence was built. But the warmth in her gaze, the raw, unfiltered emotion that poured from her, made the foundation tremble.

He saw the depth of her feelings, the genuine affection warring with the ghost of her actions. He saw the guilt that had haunted her existence, the shadow that clung to her every move. And despite everything, despite the burning rage that still consumed him, he saw a flicker of something... else. A dangerous, forbidden recognition of the connection between them. A spark, ignited by her love, that threatened to consume the carefully constructed walls of his hatred.

He knew, with a chilling certainty, that this was the moment he had dreaded. The confrontation he had both craved and feared. He could choose to succumb to the anger, to let it guide him down the path of revenge he'd so meticulously planned. Or... or he could acknowledge the impossible truth, the unwelcome realization that even amidst the ashes of his past, a fragile seed of something new, something potentially devastating, had begun to sprout.

But the hatred was still there, a gaping wound that ached with every breath.

Without a word, Aarav turned and walked inside the house.

Navya remained where she was, tears streaming silently down her face. The unspoken permission was there, hanging in the air. He hadn't told her 'yes'; he hadn't told her 'no'. He had simply left. And in that silent departure, she found a fragile space to exist – not as the woman he hated, but as the woman who loved him. The woman who would love him, even in his hatred and silence. It wasn't what she wanted, but for now, it was enough.

♡♡♡

TWENTY-NINE

A Bloom in the Desert

Things were running, if not smooth, not rough for them. Aarav continued to be indifferent towards Navya and she kept showing her love and care towards the whole family.

Aarav sat on the dinner table, reading the newspaper. Avni, ready for school, smiled at Navya, who kept a bowl of cereal in front of her.

Beside her, Aryan was shoveling spoonfuls of cereal into his mouth at an inhuman speed, his hair uncombed. The clock on the wall glared down at him, ticking away the precious minutes he didn't have.

"I am gonna be so late!" he mumbled through a mouthful of food, his eyes darting towards the clock every few seconds. "Bhabhi, can you find my Statistics book, please? I swear it hides when I need it."

"Check under the couch, Aryan," Navya said, not looking up from the teapot. "You had all your books scattered in the living room last evening."

Avni giggled.

"Bhaiya!" She called, gaining everyone's attention. "We had a career counseling session at school yesterday. They were talking about studying abroad. They made it sound so amazing."

Aarav brows knitted together in a defined frown.

"Abroad?" he repeated, the word carrying a hint of disapproval.

"Yeah," Avni said, her eyes sparkling with a sudden, unexpected urgency. "Imagine, Bhaiya, studying in London, or maybe even... California!" She paused, taking a deep breath as if daring to voice her biggest dream. "I could get into a really good university, learn so much, experience different cultures..."

Aarav shook his head.

"Avni, you are only in the ninth grade. We'll think about all of that later when the time comes. You focus on your studies here."

The flicker of hope in Avni's eyes dimmed slightly.

"But Bhaiya...I want to... I feel like there's so much more out there!"

Aryan finally found his book under the couch like Navya had said.

"She has got a point, Bhai. Bhabhi went to New York to work, right?" He turned to his brother, a teasing glint in his eyes. "What's the big deal?"

In the kitchen, the clatter of crockery suddenly stopped. Navya, a half-filled teapot in her hand, stood frozen, her gaze distant. A kaleidoscope of memories flooded her mind: the vibrant chaos of Times Square, the dizzying heights of the skyscrapers, the crisp autumn air scented with possibility, the late nights spent hunched over working under Hannah Moreau, the most successful fashion designer of that time.

"That was different, Aryan," she said while walking with her breakfast in hand. "I had a job offer and the job had its own benefits. Avni needs to focus on finishing her studies here first."

But Avni seized on Aryan's point. "But Bhabhi If you could go, why can't I?"

"I went after my graduation, Avni. We'll think about it when time comes," Navya said and looked at her,her gaze hardening.

"By the way Bhabhi," Aryan asked as he packed his college bag. "How long did you stay there?"

"Three years, I enjoyed the work so much that I never took a holiday," she paused, thinking back. "It changed me as a designer completely."

Aarav's blood turned to ice. New York... three years... shortly after graduation?

He watched her, a wave of disorientation washing over him. The familiar venom that churned within his stomach was unexpectedly replaced by a cold, hollow ache.

Aryan, oblivious to the seismic shift occurring around him, asked, "How long ago would that be?"

"Six years."

Aarav's mind went blank as the air became suffocating for him.

Aryan looked from Navya to Aarav, her brow furrowing slightly.

"Bhai, is everything alright?"

He swallowed hard, the question catching in his throat. He had to speak and voice the impossible thought that was now tearing through his mind, but his voice stuck in his throat.

"What..." he finally managed, his voice rough, barely a whisper. He had to force himself to say it. "What year did you graduate?"

Navya turned to him, sensing something was off.

"2018?"

His mind raced. *2018. Five years ago. New York. The accident.*

The carefully constructed narrative he had held onto for months crumbled into dust. The anger, the resentment, the bone-deep hatred he had nurtured for Navya – it all seemed meaningless, a distorted mistake.

He finally met her gaze, and for the first time in their six months of marriage, he didn't see a monster. Instead, he saw confusion, concern, and a hint of fear. He saw Navya, the woman he had married, the woman he had been punishing for crimes that may be she... she hadn't...

His parents' death was 5 years ago. If she was in New York at that time, then how could she...

The realisation slammed into him with the force of a physical blow.

Aarav's gaze shifted. Did he unjustly punish someone who was innocent? Months. Months of cruel words, of cold silences, of deliberate neglect. Months that she had endured silently bearing the brunt of his misplaced rage.

He remembered the nights he had watched her cry herself to sleep, the times when he had deliberately withdrawn his affection, the way he had made her feel like she was less than nothing. Each act, each word, now felt like a physical wound he had inflicted on her. He had convinced himself that she was to blame, that by hurting her, he was somehow honoring his parents' memory.

He didn't realise when he became a monster in all the rage. He, the man who had vowed to love and cherish her, had become her tormentor. The man who had promised to protect her had become the source of her pain.

The picture he had painted of Navya in his head was now shattered. He could see her as she truly was - a patient woman who had loved him unconditionally, even when he had given her nothing but cruelty in return. He had seen her resilience, her quiet dignity, as she endured his wrath. He hadn't understood then. He hadn't been willing to.

Now, the image of his parents flashed in his mind, and the realization that he had betrayed their memory by allowing his grief to turn him into something so vile burned him to the core. He could almost hear them, their voices filled with disappointment.

He didn't know what to do next. He only knew that the ground beneath his feet had just given way, and he was falling fast.

But if Navya was not at fault, then he wanted to find out the one who was actually responsible for his parents' death.

THIRTY

Bridges Burned?

The weight of his accusation had been Aarav's constant companion for the last six months. He had built a wall of resentment, a fortress of blame, with Navya's face as the only target. He had seen her silence as guilt, her tears as manipulation, her every move a confirmation of his own twisted narrative.

But now, he found himself looking at Navya with a new perspective. He watched her taking care of the house, and career, both together. She was a responsible woman. And she wouldn't have let go of it if she was behind the accident.

While Navya was asleep, her soft, even breaths filling the quiet room, Aarav pulled out all the evidence he had collected that pointed everything toward Navya being the culprit. He read through them all, each word now scrutinized, dissected, and re-evaluated. He pored over the accident report, the witness statements, and the photographs. He even found the police officer's contact information. It was a long shot, but he needed to hear it from someone who had been present, someone who wasn't influenced.

Navya stirred as the morning light hit her face, her hand instinctively reaching for the empty space beside her. Aarav, as usual, was already gone. Usually, that prompted a sigh of relief – but this morning, there was a strange void.

She stretched, pushing herself up, and noticed a small, rectangular object on her bedside table. It was a book. 'The Secret Admirer' her mind supplied instantly. Frowning, she picked it up, her fingers tracing the title. Beneath it lay a small, folded piece of paper.

Her heart quickened, a flutter of something almost new. She carefully unfolded it; the paper was thick, and slightly textured, the kind of paper she knew Aarav used for his sketches. Written in his usually sharp, bold hand, was a single sentence: "I remembered you mentioning this. Thought you might like it.'

Navya's breath hitched. She couldn't believe that Aarav had remembered the name of her favorite author and had gone through huge lengths to get a first copy of his new book.

A slow smile spread across her lips. It was a tentative thing, like a fragile bloom pushing through hard earth. She ran a finger over the note again. It felt so endearing.

Downstairs, Navya saw Aarav and Aryan at the breakfast table. Usually, he would have left for the office by the time she was ready. Taking a deep breath, she walked towards him, the novel in her hand. She had planned on starting it while waiting for her breakfast.

"Good morning, Bhabhi!" Aryan chirped, his voice a little too loud for the relatively calm atmosphere. "You're just in time. We were about to decide whether to start without you."

Navya offered a small, polite smile.

"Good morning, Aryan. Where is Avni?" she asked as she walked to sit beside him.

"Navya, don't!" Aarav screamed, making both Aryan and Navya startled.

"What happened?" Both asked in unison, Aryan dropping the coffee and Navya standing up straight.

"Nothing," he shrugged. "You were about to sit in Avni's spot. But you know that's for the princess when she will grace us with her presence. This one," he nudged the chair next to him with his foot, "is for you." He added.

Aryan laughed while Navya's jaws dropped to the ground. Aarav was actually asking her to sit beside him. She walked towards Aarav with small steps.

He smiled at her.

He smiled. Navya couldn't help the butterflies that flew in her stomach. She sat beside him and placed the novel on the table.

The moment he saw the book on her table, a strange mix of anticipation and anxiety filled Aarav. Why had he even bothered to buy it? A small voice in his head told him that he was growing soft. Even remembering her mentioning the book was a surprise. He had spent the entire night trying to rationalize that purchase.

Navya opened the book and began to read, partly because she couldn't resist and partly to control her racing heartbeat.

As he watched her, a confusing mix of emotions swirled within Aarav. He had intended to dismiss buying the book for her as a careless gesture. But now, seeing her with it, seeing the slight blush on her cheeks, he felt a strange tug in his chest. It was unsettling, but he didn't mind this unfamiliar sensation. It was something else, something different, he had never experienced before.

He shook his head, trying to dispel the feeling. He must be losing his mind, he told himself.

But the air in the house felt different, lighter, after that day. Navya, accustomed to the brittle chill of Aarav's disdain, found him glancing at her at times. The change had begun subtly and a few weeks later, Navya realised that he had stopped the clipped, accusatory tone. Instead, his interactions had become almost normal.

He had started greeting her good morning, something he hadn't done since their marriage. He even got a room in the house ready for her to work in. Navya, whose heart had been encased in ice for months, found a strange warmth blooming within her, like tiny shoots of spring emerging after the cold winter. But along with it came a gnawing unease. She couldn't understand what had triggered this. Was it a trick? A new form of torture? Was he mocking her? Was this a new tactic in his cruel game? But he hadn't said anything cruel or hurt her for a few days.

"Don't wait for me, Navya," Aarav said one evening. "I will have dinner on my way home."

His voice was surprisingly soft. Navya looked at him as he studied his reflection in the mirror.

"What are you doing?" She finally asked, her voice barely above a whisper.

He stopped looking at her through the mirror.

"Getting ready to catch up with a friend," he frowned.

"Aarav," she began slowly, her heart pounding against her ribs. "Why are you being like this?

He turned. His eyes, usually so cold and distant, held a flicker of something that she couldn't decipher. Regret? Confusion? Maybe... guilt?

"I have been... thinking," he admitted, his voice a low rumble. "About a lot of things. About what happened... about everything."

He paused, walking towards her, and knelt opposite her, making Navya stop breathing for a moment.

"I have been focusing on the wrong things, Navya. I... I have been so blinded by pain that I didn't see... I didn't see anything at all."

This was it. This was the first hint of acknowledgment that she had heard from him. This was a crack in the wall of accusations he had erected between them.

"What do you... mean?" she dared to ask, her voice trembling.

Aarav took a deep breath.

"Just give me some time. I am looking into something. And I feel we are going to be fine."

He finally met her eyes, and for the first time in what felt like an eternity, Navya could see a glimmer of sincerity behind the pain. Hope, fragile as a newborn bird, began to flutter in her chest.

"Why do you need to keep everything a secret?" Navya frowned. "Just tell me what it is, and we could look into it together."

Aarav smiled, and his hand, calloused yet gentle, cupped her cheek, and she felt a shiver chase down her spine. Time seemed to slow to a crawl, every heartbeat a drumbeat in the silence.

Navya's hand found his, her fingers intertwining with his. The simple contact sent a jolt of electricity through them both. She tilted her head up, her gaze locking with his. At that moment, the world outside the room ceased to exist. There was only the soft rhythm of their breaths, the racing of their hearts, and the undeniable pull that drew them closer.

Aarav's hand moved from her cheek to cradle the back of her neck, his thumb gently stroking the soft skin beneath her ear. He could feel the slight tremble in her frame, a mirror of his own unsteady nerves.

He closed the distance slowly, involuntarily. His heart thundered in his ears, overshadowing everything else. He felt the soft brush of her breath against his face, a teasing whisper promising more. He was so close now, he could feel the heat radiating from her. He could almost...

But a shrill, insistent ring shattered the delicate spell. Aarav's phone, lying innocently on the bedside table, wailed its digital tune. They both startled, pulling back slightly.

He sighed, running a hand through his hair, the tension from the moment still hanging in the air. The shrill ringing continued, its persistent demand an unwelcome intruder. He glanced at the screen.

Before receiving the call, he said to Navya, "I'll be back by midnight."

Navya looked at him, her cheeks flushed. She couldn't believe what she felt moments ago. Her heart felt like it might burst out of her chest, a flutter of anxious joy. But what she heard next from Aarav, burst her bubble.

"Yes, Samaira," Aarav spoke on the phone as he left the room. "I'll be reaching in 15 minutes."

THIRTY-ONE

THE COST OF INDIFFERENCE

Navya walked inside the house after a tiring day. To her surprise, she was welcomed by Aarav, who was moving towards her with a glass of water.

"How was your day?" Aarav asked, as he took her purse and kept it on the sofa.

Navya took a sip of the water.

"Fine," she replied, her tone neutral.

Aarav's smile faltered, a flicker of hurt crossing his face.

"Is everything okay?"

"I am fine, Aarav," she said, turning to face him, her expression devoid of the usual warmth.

It was a lie, and Aarav knew it.

"Navya," he said, reaching for her hand. His touch had always been something she had longed for, but now, her skin barely registered it. "I know I haven't been the best husband. But I... I am trying to change things between us. I really am."

Navya didn't pull away, but her hand remained limp in his. She met his gaze, and for a moment, Aarav thought he saw a flash of something in her eyes – not love, not anger, but weariness. It was as if she was tired of fighting, tired of hoping.

"Trying isn't enough, Aarav," Navya stated flatly. She finally pulled her hand away and walked towards the room. "You are doing all the things that you think I want. Saying good morning, offering water... it's like you are following a checklist. It doesn't feel real."

Aarav's words caught in his throat. He had done the research and had Googled. He had thought, hoped, that she would notice.

He watched as Navya walked into the room. He stood there, feeling the hollowness of her absence, even when she was just a few steps away.

He knew he had hurt her, deeply. He had taken her love for granted, and now, when he was trying to be good to her, it seemed she no longer wanted it. He had, unintentionally, shown her that his actions came out of guilt and not because of respect for her. It was like the well of affection she had once held for him had dried up, leaving behind a vast, echoing emptiness.

Later, when he entered the room, he found her in front of the mirror, removing her earrings.

"Navya," he said softly, his voice laced with hurt.

She turned, meeting his gaze in the mirror. For a moment, she saw a glimmer of the man she had fallen in love with. But the feeling was fleeting. She looked back to the mirror, removing the last earring.

"I am sleepy, Aarav," she said in a clipped and distant voice.

She slipped into bed, turning her back to him as the lights were turned off. The silence in the room was heavy, charged with unspoken questions and unacknowledged hurts. Aarav lay on his side of the bed, staring at the ceiling. He knew something had changed. He could feel the wall she had built, a barrier far more impenetrable than the one he had created for her. The more he tried, the further away she seemed to drift, and the irony of it all was almost unbearable. He had finally started to see her, but now she seemed to be looking anywhere but at him. He felt lost.

Aarav sat in his office, shocked. He had been piecing together the puzzle for a couple of months now. He was so close and he knew he would find his parents' real culprit soon but what his private investigator had shown him now, shocked him to his very core.

He stared at the grainy photo Mishra, the private investigator, had sent him. It was CCTV footage from the investigator's office that showed Navya handing a thick envelope to Mishra.

"Your wife tried to buy me out," had echoed in his mind all evening.

Aarav's hand clenched into a fist, the paper crumpling in his grip.

He pushed back his chair, the wood scraping against the floor like a scream. He had to confront her. He had to know why. The rational part of him insisted it must be a mistake, a twisted misunderstanding. But the image, so clear in its damning simplicity, gnawed at his gut.

Aarav walked inside Navya's office as she was busy measuring the cloth on the mannequin. He moved towards her, and held her by the arm, shocking her. He looked at her with rage, while she was confused seeing him in her boutique during work hours. His grip was so tight that it started hurting her.

"Aarav," Navya hissed in pain. "What are you doing?"

"You tried to bribe him, Navya." Aarav ground out, his voice a low growl. "You actually tried to pay off my private investigator."

He let go of her abruptly. Each word felt like a shard of glass scraping against his throat.

Navya's expression changed. She took out a deep breath and met his gaze head-on.

"He was wasting your time."

"Wasting my time? Or getting too close to something kept hidden?" Aarav stepped towards her, the distance shrinking between them like the fuse of a bomb. His heart hammered against his ribs, mixing fear and betrayal into an agonizing cocktail. "Did you think I wouldn't find out?"

"Aarav, I think you are too obsessed with all this."

"Obsessed? I want to find my parents' killer! Can you honestly, with a straight face, call that an obsession?" He spat out the words, his control slipping, anger bubbling over.

"You already know the truth, Aarav. You have always known. What more do you want to find out?"

Aarav staggered back.

"Navya..."

Navya took a deep breath.

"Why waste time and money digging into something you already know?" she continued, her voice softening ever so slightly. It made the words even more chilling. "There's no mystery, is there? You know who was responsible for your parents' deaths."

The blood drained from Aarav's face.

"Are you... really.. accepting..." he managed, his voice barely louder than a whisper.

"A hint is enough for the wise," she whispered. "You will not find anything new, Aarav. It's all what you have already known."

Aarav ran a hand through his hair, feeling the tremors coursing through his limbs. He struggled to find purchase in her words, desperate to find a flaw, a hidden lie. He knew she was lying.

He laughed, a short, harsh bark devoid of mirth.

"I know I have been blaming you for months. But it's all absurd. You were in New York. You were thousands of miles away. Why are you doing this?"

"It doesn't matter where I was," she insisted, her voice rising in pitch, tinged with desperation. "I did it, Aarav! I am... I am the one."

Navya paced, her movements frantic and jerky, the plush carpet offering no solace beneath her restless feet. Each denial from Aarav felt like an agonizing cut, making it harder to maintain her composure.

"Stop it, Navya! Just stop!" Aarav's voice was a sharp crack, making her halt, her body trembling. He moved closer, his gaze fixed on her. "Do you think I am an idiot?"

"I was here for the holidays," she said, turning her gaze.

"You had said you never took a holiday while working there."

Navya's breath hitched.

"When I was pleading that I wasn't responsible for it, you kept accusing me. And now that I am accepting all your accusations, why can't you just believe me?"

"What kind of a fool do you take me for, Navya?" He grabbed her arms, his grip tight, his knuckles white. "Do you really think I would believe this? This... this utter nonsense you are sprouting?"

He let go of her and turned away, running his hands through his hair again, a gesture of pure frustration and despair.

"I don't know why you are doing this, but I'll find out."

The sound of the door slamming echoed through the hollow corridor followed by his retreating footsteps.

THIRTY-TWO
The Revelation

The air in the Oberoi household's small apartment crackled with anticipation. Balloons bobbed against the ceiling, their vibrant colors contrasting the growing tension in the room. Navya sat at the edge of the sofa and kept glancing at her watch. Her sister, Kavya, a whirlwind of vibrant energy in a bright pink dress, flitted from the table laden with cake and snacks, to the window and peered out into the darkening street.

"He's going to miss the cake cutting," Kavya fretted for what felt like the hundredth time. "Less than 10 minutes left to strike 12!"

"He'll be here, Kavya Dee," Avni said, admiring the cake.

Navya, however, felt a familiar knot tighten in her stomach. Aarav had to come, or else Kavya would be heartbroken.

"It's such a simple thing, being on time," Kavya muttered, echoing Navya's unspoken thoughts. She knew that Navya had been struggling, trying to bridge the growing chasm in her marriage with everything she had.

Finally, a car door slammed outside. Kavya gasped and rushed towards the window, her face lighting up.

"He's here! He's finally here!"

Aarav strode into the house, his tie loosened and hair slightly disheveled. He looked tired, but his eyes softened when he saw Kavya, a genuine smile spreading across his face.

"Happy birthday, my favorite!" He swept her into a hug, presenting a beautifully wrapped gift.

Kavya giggled, the earlier anxiety melting away.

"You're late, as usual!" she said, playfully punching his arm.

"I wouldn't miss it for the world," Aarav replied, his gaze catching Navya's across the room. His smile faltered for a moment, replaced by a forced one.

"Jiju, come on, let's cut the cake now!" Kavya urged, grabbing his arm and pulling him towards the table.

As Aarav settled beside her, Navya couldn't help but watch him. He looked genuinely happy, laughing with Kavya and her other cousins. He was so good with her sister, so naturally affectionate. Her heart ached.

They sang the birthday song as Kavya cut the cake. The room then buzzed with conversation and music. Navya felt a gentle nudge on her arm. It was Aarav.

"I am sorry, I was late," he said. His voice was low and almost hesitant.

Navya, taken aback, replied. "Kavya would have been heartbroken if you hadn't come."

"I will never break anyone's heart ever again," he said with raw honesty, which made her heart skip a beat.

They fell into an uneasy silence, surrounded by the joyful chaos of the party. It was as if they were standing on the edge of something, unsure whether to step forward or back away.

"Excuse me," she muttered and walked away to join her cousins. Aarav kept looking at her with a smile on his face.

"Aarav," Anjali Oberoi's voice brought him out of the trance. "Thanks a lot for coming, beta."

He saw Navya's parents walking towards him.

"Aunty, Uncle," he said, his voice calm but firm, cutting through the party chatter. "Could I have a word with you? In private?"

Rajesh's smile faltered, and Anjali's hand flew to her throat, in a nervous flutter.

"Of course, but... is everything alright?" Rajesh asked, his voice a little too low-pitched.

"I just have a question I need to ask," He gestured toward a small study tucked away behind the living room, a room filled with the scent of old books. They followed him, their steps hesitant.

He shut the door gently but firmly behind them, a click that sounded like a death knell in the quiet room. He turned to them, his back against the door, his arms crossed over his chest. He was no longer the affable son-in-law, but a man in search of truth.

He met their eyes, his own holding a chilling resolve.

"I want to know why," he started, his voice low and even, "Why did you bribe the police?"

Rajesh paled, his face draining of color, while Anjali gasped, her eyes widening in terror. Her hand flew to her mouth as if to stifle the words that threatened to spill out.

"Aarav... we..." Rajesh stammered, his voice trembling.

"Don't even try to lie to me," Aarav said, his voice clipped. "Not anymore. The police report from the night of the accident... was falsified. Rewritten. Someone paid to make sure no name was on it at all. I now know that it was you both."

He watched as the color completely drained from their faces, leaving them ashen. The denial began, stumbling and weak, but Aarav held his ground.

Anjali broke down first, tears streaming down her face.

"It was for her, Aarav! We... We wanted to protect her. She was so young... We did what we thought was best for her."

"Aarav!" The three of them heard a voice call out and turned to look at the intruder. Navya was standing near the door, her breath heavy.

"They don't need to give you an explanation," she said as she walked towards them. She couldn't bear the sight of her parents crying. "How could you do this to my parents?

"They do need to explain themselves, Navya," Aarav crossed his arms. "The people who died that day were my parents."

Navya looked away, unable to meet his eyes.

"You know, Navya, Even if you tried to fail my attempts to find the truth, I have been doing some digging. I know who you're covering for."

Navya's eyes widened for a fleeting moment, the impassive mask cracking slightly.

"What... what are you talking about?"

He pressed on, seeing the flicker of fear in her eyes.

"Someone else was involved, someone very close to you, wasn't it?" He watched her reaction closely.

Navya's hands curled into fists.

"Stop it, Aarav," her voice trembled, laced with fear that finally replaced her cold exterior. "Stop it! You can't do this!"

Aarav raised an eyebrow, playing the innocent.

"Do what? I'm just trying to understand. If you're taking the blame for someone, I am simply trying to find out who that person is."

She stepped back, her gaze darting to the door as if looking for an escape.

"Don't... don't you dare," she stammered, her voice cracking. "Don't you dare torture her the way you tortured me? She doesn't deserve it. She was young. She didn't know what she was doing!"

The words struck him like a physical blow.

"She?" he asked, his voice barely a whisper.

"It was me," They turned and saw Kavya standing, tears filled in her eyes.

THIRTY-THREE

SHATTERED ILLUSIONS

"It was me," they turned and saw Kavya standing, tears filled in her eyes.

Navya's eyes filled with desperate pain.

"Please, just leave her alone! It's all my fault, just leave my sister out of it. Please, Aarav, you have hated me all these months... You have tortured me, but I can't bear to see her at the receiving end of your wrath."

The room spun. Aarav had expected a name and a confession of collusion, may be of Mr or Mrs. Oberoi but not her. Not Kavya. The pieces of the puzzle, fractured and distorted, began to slide into a new, even more horrifying configuration.

The truth crashed against Aarav like a rogue wave.

He sank onto the cold, stone floor of the study.

Navya looked at him, his eyes wide with a terrifying mix of disbelief and fear. She kept glancing at Kavya, then back at Aarav, unable to anticipate either of the two's next reaction..

Anjali's body shook with grief. Rajesh sat slumped in his chair, his gaze fixed on the floor, his hand pressed against his forehead as if attempting to hold back the pain that threatened to engulf him.

"It...it wasn't intentional," Kavya whispered, her voice barely audible. "It was an accident. A terrible, horrible accident." Her words were punctuated by gasps, each one a sharp intake of breath that seemed to cause her physical pain.

Aarav's world tilted on its axis. His head spun. He stared at her, the girl he had admired, the one who was nothing less than a sister to him, had just confessed the truth.

It wasn't just a confession; it was a brutal blow.

His mind raced, trying to grab hold of a logical explanation, a plausible reason, an alternative reality. How could the gentle, innocent Kavya, do something so horrific?

He felt a dizzying mix of emotions. Disbelief warred with a creeping horror. Hurt, sharp and agonizing, clawed at his throat.

He looked at her again, searching for some sign of remorse, some explanation that could begin to unravel the mess she had created. He saw her watching him, her face a mask of anxiety, but the innocence he thought he had seen for years was now replaced by an uncomfortable guilt.

His vision blurred.

"Kavya was just fifteen," Mr. Rajesh Oberoi stammered, his face etched with shame. "She took the car without our permission. It was raining heavily, and she lost control. We were terrified. We knew we had to protect her."

"We bribed the police," Anjali added, her voice barely a croak. "We paid the media. We suppressed the story. We... we wanted to protect her."

Kavya flinched, her face crumpling.

"I am sorry, Jiju. I was... I was stupid. I know I don't deserve forgiveness.." she looked up at Aarav, pleading with his eyes. "I am so sorry. I should have come forward sooner."

Aarav stared at her. He saw a woman burdened by a secret she could no longer bear.

"It was Kavya who Navya was trying to protect," Rajesh said. "We all wanted to protect her."

That is why she didn't want him to investigate.

Aarav stood up, pushing his hands through his hair. The weight of their confession settled on him, a heavy burden he wasn't sure he could ever bear. The silence in the room was now different, no longer filled with nervous anticipation, but rather, with the chilling weight of truth finally unearthed. He looked at Navya. Her eyes screamed of guilt, regret, and fear. He couldn't stand there any longer. Without a word, he left the room and then the house.

Aarav wandered on the street aimlessly.

He remembered all the evidence that his sources had provided, pointing to Rajesh Oberoi's daughter. He had thought it was Navya who was responsible for his parents' death. He had accepted it as the truth. It wasn't Navya. It was Kavya. Kavya had been behind the wheel. A fifteen-year-old girl, terrified and reckless, had been the actual culprit, and Navya, his wife, had taken the fall to protect her.

He felt a sickening swirl of guilt churning in his stomach. He remembered Navya's sudden adamant confession about the accident and her enduring his coldness without ever complaining. She was protecting her sister. But why didn't she tell him the truth? His breath quickened as he realized she had never trusted him to understand the truth because he had overlooked her unwavering love and support in his misguided rage. He had taken her for granted, blaming her for a tragedy that was not her fault.

A wave of remorse washed over him. He longed to make amends, to apologize for the pain he had inflicted. But how could he ever truly atone for the injustice he had done?

His heart ached with a longing to see Navya. He had to seek her forgiveness. But fear gnawed at him. What if she rejected his apology and spurned his attempts at reconciliation? He had wronged her beyond measure; he deserved her contempt.

Yet, amidst the despair, a glimmer of hope remained. He knew he had to face Navya, own his mistakes, and beg for her understanding. He owed her that much.

As soon as Navya saw Aarav enter the room, she rushed to him.

"Aarav... please..." she croaked, her voice trembling and eyes clouded with a paralyzing dread. "Please, don't... don't do to her what you... what you did to me."

Her words came out in a ragged rush, a torrent of desperate pleas. She reached out a trembling hand towards him, a gesture that was both begging and pleading for understanding.

"She... she was so young. It was an accident, Aarav, a terrible accident! She never meant to... She was just a fifteen-year-old kid..." Navya's voice broke, and she could barely speak the last few words. "Please... please, understand."

Her plea was a desperate attempt to shield Kavya. She had endured his torment, his coldness, his cruelty, telling herself she deserved it, that it was a small price to pay to keep her sister safe. But now, that was all shattered. The thought of Kavya enduring even a fraction of what she had been through ripped through her with a visceral pain.

Her breathing grew shallower, more rapid. Her vision began to blur. The sounds around her seemed to fade, replaced by the roaring in her ears. The world narrowed down to the pounding in her chest and the suffocating tightness in her throat. A wave of dizziness washed over her, and she swayed, nearly collapsing.

Aarav, who had been in a mix of emotions, was taken aback. All his way home, he had kept imagining this moment, the confrontation, his helplessness, and also an intense argument. But he hadn't imagined this - Navya's desperate terror.

He watched Navya, her face pale, her body trembling uncontrollably. He saw the panic in her eyes, the sheer, unyielding fear. He saw the weight she had carried, a burden she had taken on herself to protect her younger sister. He saw the sacrifices she had made, the pain she had endured.

"Navya?" He walked towards her.

She tried to speak, but only a strangled sound escaped her lips. Her breathing grew more rapid and shallow, and he noticed small tremors running through her body. He moved closer, a hand instinctively reaching out to touch her arm, but he hesitated. He didn't know what to do. He had seen her frustrated, upset, even angry, but never like this.

"Are you okay, Navya?" he asked in a slightly shaky voice. He hated the helplessness he felt. He hated not knowing how to make her feel better.

Tears welled in her eyes, spilling down her cheeks like tiny waterfalls. She shook her head, her chest still rising and falling in frantic, uneven breaths.

Aarav reached out, this time carefully taking her hand. Her skin was cold and clammy. He squeezed gently.

"Okay, okay, Navya. It's alright. You're okay. Just breathe with me, okay?"

He took a deep, exaggerated breath, holding it for a moment, and then slowly released it, hoping she would follow. Navya remained in her chaotic rhythm, her eyes darting frantically around the room as if searching for an escape.

"It's alright," he repeated, his voice softer now, laced with a newfound understanding. He moved closer, sliding onto the bed beside her. He gently pulled her into a hug. She was stiff at first, resisting the embrace, but he held her firm, whispering soothing words against her hair.

"You are safe, Navya. I am here. You're okay," He continued to breathe slowly and deeply, hoping the rhythm would seep into her. He felt the tension slowly ebb from her body, her frantic breaths becoming slightly more measured.

He knew he needed to ground her, to bring her back to the present.

"Can you feel my hand?" He took her hand in his hand and gently rubbed his thumb over her knuckles. "Can you feel how warm it is?"

She nodded faintly, her focus slowly starting to return to him.

"Can you hear me?" he asked, his voice still low and calm.

Another tiny nod.

"Good," He pulled back a little, enough to look at her face. "Look at me, Navya. It's okay. Just look at me."

He could see the fear still clinging to her eyes, but it was less intense now. He continued to talk to her softly, his voice a steady anchor in the storm raging within her.

Slowly, painstakingly, the color began to return to her cheeks. Her breathing became less shallow, less erratic. The tremors subsided. The tears eventually stopped, leaving behind red, swollen eyes.

He held her in his arms, rocking her gently until she was finally calm. She leaned against him, exhausted, her head resting on his chest. He could feel the frantic beat of her heart gradually slowing down to a normal rhythm.

They stayed like that for a long time, the silence comfortable and reassuring. As the night darkened, the two found solace in each other's arms.

THIRTY-FOUR

DISTANCE AND DECISIONS

The air in the airport's international terminal was like a blanket of farewells. Aarav's heart hammered against his ribs as he scanned the crowded departure hall, his eyes wide and desperate. He had been late again.

He had found her note this morning, tucked beneath a ceramic elephant on their bedside table.

"By the time you read this, we will be gone," it had said, the words stark and final. "I can't do this anymore, Aarav. We want some stability."

He had understood the "we". She had taken Kavya with her to protect her. He couldn't understand how to tell her how he felt. He had raced to the airport, fueled by a frantic hope that perhaps, just perhaps, he wasn't too late.

Navya clutched the handle of her small handbag. Her free hand worried the strap of her purse, as she sat in the car, outside the airport.

She checked her watch for the tenth time in as many minutes. Gate 42. Boarding in thirty minutes. Good. She had no wish to linger. Every moment spent in this city felt like a pinprick to her already bruised heart.

Ten months. Ten months of indifference, hurt, tears, and hatred. Now that Aarav had known the truth, all of his rage was going to fall upon Kavya. She couldn't let her sister go through what she had. She didn't trust Aarav. He was too blinded with vengeance. She couldn't risk it. She sent Kavya to the security point, ahead of her, while she hung back, sending out all the emergency emails and messages that needed to be sent before she boarded.

She was going to reset everything, but her heart. Her thumb hovered over Aarav's name in her phone contacts. She had left just a note, keeping it as brief and impersonal as possible.

Just as she moved out of the car, a figure jostled through the crowd, his rapid stride and panicked expression unmistakable even from a distance. Aarav.

Her breath hitched. Her heart, traitorous that it was, leaped into a frantic rhythm. Why was he here?

He stopped abruptly opposite her, panting slightly, his eyes wide and searching, his dark hair disheveled. He looked like he had been running for miles. The usually composed, meticulously dressed Aarav looked...vulnerable.

He pushed through the throng of people, his eyes darting between families hugging tearful goodbyes and business travellers tapping away on their phones. He was out of breath, sticky with sweat, his crisp white shirt now crumpled and stained.

Navya walked towards the main gate, her head down. She didn't want to be weak in front of him.

Aarav surged forward, calling out her name, his voice cracking with an emotion he hadn't allowed himself to feel in years.

"Navya! Navya, please, wait!"

She stopped, her shoulders stiffening. She didn't look back.

"Navya, please," he pleaded, reaching her in a few strides. He reached for her arm, but she flinched away as if he'd burned her. "Don't go."

She finally turned towards him, her eyes mirroring his own pain, but laced with a steely resolve.

"Why, Aarav? So that you can get my sister arrested?" Her voice was low and controlled, but the tremor barely hidden beneath the surface betrayed her own turmoil.

"No... " He searched for the right words. Words that could undo the damage he had caused, but failed. "I would... Let's go home. We can talk about this." He begged, instead.

A flicker of pain briefly crossed her expression, but it was quickly replaced with a wall of coldness.

"Home? A Home is where there's love, respect, and kindness, Aarav. Things you have denied me."

"But we can fix this," he insisted, his voice rising. "Just listen to me once."

"It's too late, Aarav. I have made my decision," her eyes darted toward the security gate, the metallic detectors glinting under the harsh lights. "It's time for my flight."

"No!" He reached for her again, this time wrapping his fingers around her wrist, pulling her towards him. "Please, Navya, think about Aryan and Avni, what will I tell them?"

Navya tugged free, her gaze unwavering.

"Let me go, Aarav. I have talked to them. Yes, I had to lie that I am on a tour. They will not ask you about me."

He felt a sharp, painful burn behind his eyes. He opened his mouth to speak, to beg, but the words wouldn't come.

"It's time to move on."

She turned and walked towards security, leaving Aarav standing there, his hand outstretched, empty, his heart shattering into a million pieces.

"Move on? From us? From everything?"

Her resolve cracked slightly. The carefully constructed facade started to fray. She almost, almost, allowed the truth to spill out – about how her heart was still with him and she could never move away from him. But then, Kavya's innocent face pierced through. He would hurt her.

"There is no 'us', Aarav. There never was. It was always you. Only you," Navya said, her voice trembling slightly despite her efforts to keep it steady.

Navya turned. Her back was to him again, and she walked towards the gate. She didn't look back. She couldn't.

Aarav watched her walk away, each step a painful echo in the sudden silence that had fallen between them. He had seen her walk away countless times before – to work, after a fight, in anger – but this was different. This wasn't just a temporary parting; this was... a farewell. He hadn't understood it until this moment until the distance between them was growing with every measured step she took.

He had taken her presence for granted, like the air he breathed, never truly appreciating its life-giving necessity. Now, as he watched the curve of her back and the sway of her hair, he felt a hollow ache start to bloom in his chest. It was as if a vital organ had been silently removed, leaving behind a gaping wound.

He realized with a sickening lurch of his stomach, that it wasn't just her presence, that he was losing; it was her laughter, the way her eyes crinkled at the corners when she smiled, the gentle touch of her hand on his arm, the quiet strength she possessed that always grounded him. These weren't just her attributes; they were the essence of his happiness, the definition of his home. He had been so blind, so foolish.

He had been so focused on the minor flaws and on the everyday frustrations, that he had completely ignored the enormous beauty of their shared existence. And now, as she walked away, he finally understood the depth of the void she would leave, a void that he feared would never be filled. All that was left now was the bitter taste of his negligence and the excruciating knowledge that he had realized his love only when he was about to lose it.

THIRTY-FIVE

The Weight of Repentance

Aarav stood in the Oberoi living room with his fists clenched so tight his knuckles were white. Rajesh Oberoi was on the sofa, his usually jovial face pale and drawn. Anjali Oberoi, her eyes puffy and red-rimmed, wrung her hands in her lap, avoiding Aarav's gaze. The silence was in the living room harrowing. and every tick of the clock in the hallway was a miniature explosion.

"So, are you finally going to explain?" Aarav asked, his voice dangerously low. He had driven straight here from the airport. The rage, a cold, hard knot in his chest, was barely contained. "You let them go. You let my wife go away."

Rajesh finally met Aarav's eyes, shame and defiance crossing his face.

"Aarav, please, sit. Let's talk calmly."

"Calmly?" Aarav scoffed, taking a step toward them. "My wife and her sister are god knows where, probably halfway across the world, and you want me to be calm? Navya took the fall for an accident she didn't commit! And you just let it happen?"

Anjali finally spoke, her voice trembling.

"It wasn't like that, son. It...it was messy."

"Messy?!" Aarav's voice rose, the control he had been clinging to finally slipping.

"My life with her is at stake! How can you just dismiss this as just messy?" He ran a hand through his hair, the frustration threatening to consume him.

"Were you going to let Navya sacrifice herself, her marriage, her happiness, and her life for your younger daughter?" Aarav asked.

To his surprise, Rajesh stood up, anger slowly bubbling on his tired, old features.

"How dare you, Mr. Singhania!" He thundered.

Anjali sobbed more, the accusation breaking her heart.

"Do you think a parent can choose between their children? Do you think it was easy for us to let Navya take the fall? Why do you think Navya took the fall in the first place?" Rajesh asked, and Aarav was stumped.

He knew the answer, but the shame associated with it was too much. But he couldn't look away from his father-in-law's face. Despite everything, he couldn't let anyone tell the truth. He knew it, he knew he had messed up, but he also knew that the second someone else pointed it out, it would be too real for him to handle. All his anger at his in-laws for letting Navya leave seemed to have ebbed out and been replaced with guilt and shame. Rajesh, however, saw the shame reflected on his face.

"Yes, you are right. She did it because of you."

"Rajesh!" Anjali whispered. "It's between the kids, we shouldn't..."

"No, Anjali, he needs to know. Aarav, don't think we didn't notice the changes in Navya. She was never this downcast, even after her breakup. She was never a show-off, but now, everything she does is on Page 3. We first thought she was trying hard to make you happy, to adjust to your world, so we chose not to comment. After all, we have raised a smart daughter who knows when to fight and when not to, so we trusted her to fight for herself when the time came. But now we know. She was doing it all out of love, and when she found out the warped truth you told her, she did it all out of guilt," he paused. "When did you find out about the accident?"

Aarav hesitated.

"The day of the wedding."

"And you chose to marry her?" Anjali asked, confused. "Why would you want to marry your parents' supposed killer."

"Because he wanted revenge." Rajesh gritted. "When Navya had cried that day, begged us to tell the truth, and said her marriage was in shambles, I had my doubts. And I was right. I just wished I had picked up on it earlier and had protected her."

Aarav looked at his feet. The shame, the guilt, the pain, it was too much. He couldn't breathe.

"I didn't know before I married her. The private investigator called just after the wedding was over. But that's not an excuse, because I chose to stay married to her for my own selfish motives. He paused. "When did Navya know that Kavya was behind the accident?"

"Navya was investigating on her own. She was sure she wouldn't have drunken till out of senses. When she told us that she was going to surrender to the police, we had to tell her the truth," Rajesh confessed. "We didn't choose one daughter over another. It was Navya's choice. It wasn't a smart one, but she is an emotional person. She knew you would hurt Kavya, and she wanted to protect her. She was used to your hatred, but Kavya wasn't, and she wanted to shield her."

"Kavya is still going through therapy sessions," Anjali added. "She suffered PTSD after the accident. After you confronted her, her trauma was back. She changed. She is isolating herself. So Navya took Kavya along with her. We had to trust her to protect her sister."

Aarav could feel the breath leaving his lungs. He suddenly felt a wave of intense guilt wash over him. He had been so focused on his anger that he had not even seen how much pain Navya might have been in.

He looked from his father-in-law to his mother-in-law, now seeing them as strong parents who had made a choice for their daughter years ago. He would have done the same for Avni or maybe something even more. Something that would even be illegal and unethical in the world's eyes.

"Where did they go?" he asked, controlling the tears that threatened to fall at any moment.

"We can't help you," Rajesh said, determined.

Aarav's heart sank. "Please, I promise I won't hurt..."

"We have promised Navya that we will not interfere," Anjali interrupted. "So, it's better you leave."

She opened the door and gazed at the opposite wall stoically, not meeting his eyes. "Leave, Aarav."

Aarav looked from Anjali's cold, unyielding face to Rajesh's unwavering gaze. He knew arguing was futile.

He turned and walked out, the sound of the door clicking shut behind him. The hollowness in his chest increased as he realized that he had no idea where Navya was, and he had no idea what to do next. The only thing he knew was that whatever was happening, was happening because of him. And that thought was more terrifying than anything else.

But he knew he had to find Navya. He needed to beg for her forgiveness. He had to bring her back. He needed her to know that he would not let her carry another burden for anyone. He would be there to shoulder it with her. The anger had now been replaced with determination. He knew, in his heart, it was not going to be an easy task, but he was ready for the challenge. He was willing to do anything to win back his wife.

♡♡♡

THIRTY-SIX

A GLIMMER IN THE GREY

The relentless buzz of New York City was a stark contrast to the quiet dread that often settled in Navya and Kavya's small, sparsely furnished apartment in the East Village. Sunlight, sharp, sliced through the fire escape, illuminating the dust motes dancing in the air. It was a Wednesday morning, a weekday meant for bustling productivity, but the sisters moved with a languid slowness, each lost in their own world.

Navya, dressed in a loose, charcoal-colored tunic and leggings, was stitching a sample garment. The rhythmic action of pulling the needle through the fabric was a kind of meditation, a way to create something tangible in the face of the formless anxieties that haunted her. She had her portfolio spread out on the small table, showcasing her designs – bold silhouettes, innovative textiles, a clear vision that belied the uncertainty swirling within her chest. New York was supposed to be a fresh start, a blank canvas. But the brushstrokes of her past kept bleeding through, threatening to muddy the picture.

She glanced at Kavya. She sat on the floor by the window, sketching on a large sketchpad. Her brow was furrowed in concentration, but her gaze seemed unfocused, her hand moving in fits and starts. She had barely touched her breakfast, a half-eaten sandwich sitting forlornly on a plate beside her. Navya knew she hadn't slept well again – the dark circles under her eyes a testament to her restless nights.

"Kavya," Navya called out gently, her voice a low murmur. "Are you okay?"

She didn't look up.

"I am fine, Dee," she mumbled, the word a thin, brittle thing.

Navya sighed. She knew "fine" was code for "I am falling apart, but don't try to help."

She pushed aside her own anxieties and walked over, kneeling beside her.

"What are you drawing?" she asked, trying to sound casual.

Kavya hesitated, then reluctantly turned the sketchpad so she could see. It was a fragmented, chaotic sketch – a series of distorted figures, swirling lines, and faces with anguished expressions. It looked like a nightmare caught on paper.

Navya didn't comment on the unsettling drawing.

"It's... intense," she simply said.

Kavya snatched the notepad back.

"It's nothing. Just... garbage."

"It's not garbage, Kavya," Navya said softly. "It's... a reflection. It's okay to feel things, to express them."

She looked at her for a moment, the raw grief she tried so hard to conceal glinting in her eyes.

"It's not okay, Dee. It's never going to be okay," her voice cracked, and tears welled in her eyes. "I keep seeing his face. Every time I close my eyes, I see... and it's my fault."

Navya's heart clenched. She knew who Kavya was talking about. She, herself, was no better. Despite her best efforts, Navya hadn't been able to break through the wall of guilt that she had built around herself. She wrapped an arm around her shoulders, pulling her close.

"It's okay," she whispered, his voice thick with emotion. "You'll be ok. We'll be ok."

Kavya didn't respond. She leaned into her sister, her body trembling. Navya felt her pain as if it were her own. She felt the weight of the unspoken words, the unaddressed trauma that threatened to consume them both.

"This city," Kavya said after a long silence, her voice muffled against her shoulder. "It's so loud. But it's not loud enough to drown out the... the echoes," she shuddered, and Navya held her tighter.

She knew exactly what her sister meant. The city's bright lights couldn't penetrate the darkness they carried within them.

Navya knew they couldn't keep living like this. They had to find a way to heal, to move forward. But how? She looked out at the city below, the endless maze of concrete and steel, and a wave of exhaustion washed over her. She could not let Kavya drown in depression like this. She knew Kavya needed to go out, meet new people, and make new friends. Kavya needed to have a normal life.

"Come one, gather your stuff, we have to meet someone."

The house felt too big, too empty. The absence of Navya's laughter, the comforting clatter of her cooking, and the vibrant chaos she usually brought echoed in the silence of Singhania mansion. Aarav moved through the rooms like a ghost, the weight of his choices pressing down on him with every creak of the floorboards. He traced the outline of a photograph on the mantelpiece – Navya's radiant smile. He had shattered that smile, and now he was left picking up the scattered fragments of a life he had carelessly destroyed.

He had been doing this for weeks – wandering, remembering, and punishing himself. The internal battles, the fallout from his mistakes, were a constant reminder of how thoroughly he had messed up.

The aroma of Avni's famous lentil soup filled the dining room as he sat at the head of the table, a place that had once felt like a throne of power but now felt like a constant reminder of his failures. Across from him, Aryan meticulously stirred his soup, avoiding eye contact. Avni, usually the most talkative, sat quietly, her gaze flickering between her two brothers.

Aarav picked at his food, the familiar taste doing little to soothe the knot in his stomach. He had been a whirlwind of rage not so long ago, a man ruled by his impulses, making choices that had shattered the fragile bonds of his family. Now, he was a man who was trying to piece himself back together, painstakingly learning to build instead of destroy. The hardest part was accepting the wreckage he had left behind.

"I love this, Avni," he said, smiling at his little sister. "It's yum!"

"But Bhabhi makes it better," Aryan said, sipping. "I miss her."

Aarav's heart twisted. He reached out and ruffled his hair, the gesture feeling hollow even to himself.

"But I make it exactly how she taught me," Avni frowned. "I hope she is back soon. She doesn't tell me where she is and keeps saying she is just traveling. She doesn't even post anything anymore."

Aarav sighed. Navya had been in touch with his sibling but hadn't revealed her whereabouts. She must know he would squeeze it out of them.

"You know," Aryan said, his eyes widening, "I think I saw something... kind of like a clue, maybe?"

Aarav's head snapped up, and a flicker of something akin to hope sparked in his chest.

"A clue?"

Aryan pulled out his phone, his fingers swiping across the screen.

"I saw a post on Instagram. Kavya was tagged."

Avni gasped and leaned over to look at the phone. Aarav's heart hammered against his ribs. He waited, barely breathing, as Aryan navigated to the post.

"It's a post from their cousin from New York," Aryan informed and Avni nodded. "The one we met at Bhai and Bhabhi's wedding."

There it was. A photo of Kavya with a group of people. She was smiling, but Aarav could see the burden she had behind that smile. Behind her, a flash of bright yellow – a taxi, unmistakably from New York City.

"She is partying!" Avni commented. "While Bhabhi is working."

"So what?" Aryan frowned. "I party while Bhai works."

The two younger siblings bickered, but Aarav kept staring at the picture, his eyes drinking in every detail. It was Kavya. She was in New York. So, Navya was in New York. Why had he not thought of it before? How could he be so stupid? She had stayed there for years, so it was the best place for Navya to move to.

For the first time in weeks, a genuine hope lit up Aarav's eyes. He might have destroyed his own happiness, but perhaps, just perhaps, he could still salvage the pieces.

The anxiety in Aarav's cabin felt too large and cold. He hadn't slept properly in weeks because the image of Navya's face, that last look of profound sadness in her eyes, had kept haunting him. He swallowed the knot of panic in his throat and looked at his PR team – Tanya, the sharp, no-nonsense strategist; Matthew, his social media manager; and Maya, the calm and collected media liaison. He had summoned them urgently, bypassing their usual schedules and project briefings.

"Thank you for coming on such short notice," Aarav began, his voice rougher than he intended. He ran a hand through his already disheveled hair. "This is... different. It is not our usual campaign."

Tanya leaned forward curiously while the other two shared a look of intrigue.

Aarav took a deep breath.

"It's...personal. I need your help to find my wife."

The silence in the room was thick enough to cut with a knife. Mathew's fingers hovered over his laptop and Maya's eyes widened with surprise. Tanya's stylus froze midair. They were used to crafting narratives and managing perceptions, but this was a request that fell far outside their professional remit.

"Navya," he continued, his gaze fixed on the table. "She left a few weeks ago. I...I haven't been able to reach her. I have tried everything," His voice cracked, and he immediately straightened, pushing down the vulnerability that threatened to overwhelm him. "She might be in New York. Her cousin lives there, and Navya also worked there for three years. That's... that's all I know."

Mathew coughed, breaking the silence.

"Aarav, with all due respect, this is not really our forte. Also, this is your private matter..."

"I know," Aarav interrupted, his voice tight. "Believe me, I know. But you are the best at finding information. You have handled messier business scandals and swayed public opinion with a few well-placed tweets. You are experts in tracking down information that is impossible to find. I need that now." He looked at them, his eyes pleading. "Please, it's a request."

Maya, her usual calm giving way to empathy, spoke softly.

"We understand, sir. But we are not investigators. We handle public image, not private matters. You should contact a private detective."

Aarav nodded, knowing he was asking the impossible. But he was running out of options. "Think of it as a particularly challenging campaign. Navya is the target audience. We need to reach her, to find her. Her cousin's name is Suhana Oberoi. She lives in New York, I think. I don't have her address."

He fidgeted through his phone and opened the screenshot of the image that Aryan had sent to him. The room fell silent as each of them silently looked at the picture.

"That's it," Aarav said. "I just have this picture of Kavya for you to work with," he said as he pointed at the photo.

Tanya, pitying his desperation, took a deep breath.

"Okay, Aarav," she said slowly, her gaze unwavering. "We'll see what we can do. Guys, consider this... an unconventional job. Matthew, look for Suhana Oberoi in New York with any connection to Navya or to Kavya. Maya, you can contact your sources in New York in the fashion industry as I feel Navya might have approached some fashion designer or brand for a job as moving her label there seems unlikely, given the lengths she has gone to be anonymous and starting a brand new one takes time, investment and most importantly, connections."

Mathew and Maya nodded, their usual professional composure returning but with an added layer of solemnity. They understood the urgency in Aarav's voice, the raw pain that thrummed beneath the surface.

Aarav wasn't just their client this time. He was a man desperate to bring his wife home. He offered a small, grateful smile. He knew it was a long shot, but it was the only shot he had left. He would not fail. He couldn't.

He pulled out his phone and texted his siblings.

"Pack your bags, kids. We are going to New York."

THIRTY-SEVEN
THE HUNT

Aarav stood on a busy corner in Greenwich Village, the cacophony of New York City hurting his ears. Beside him stood Aryan, tired, from the long flight, and Avni, her eyes admiring the city with awe.

"Bhai," Aryan asked as he yawned. "We have come here, but how will we find Bhabhi?"

"Yes," Avni said, still admiring her surroundings. "How would we surprise her if we don't know where she is?"

"If we have arrived, then we will find her too," Aarav said with determination. "Let's go to the hotel first."

An hour later, Aarav sat hunched in a dingy corner of a café, the aroma of burnt coffee a bitter reminder of his dwindling patience. Aryan and Avni had hit the bed right after breakfast, but he was trying to find a way to search for Navya.

His eyes kept darting to his phone, begging it to vibrate or to flash with a notification. But it remained dark, adding to his frustration.

He closed his eyes, picturing Navya's face. He saw the curve of her wide, expressive eyes, how her brow furrowed when she was concentrating, the soft blush that would creep onto her cheeks when she laughed.

How would she react when they finally met?

His mind raced, picturing a thousand different scenarios. He imagined her confused and eyes wide with bewilderment. He imagined her feeling nervous. And then, he wanted to hold her, reassure her and show her that he was here and would make everything okay. He pictured himself taking her hand, his thumb stroking her skin, offering a comfort that transcended words. He needed to see her, for her to know that he loved her.

He desperately wished he had the power to fast-forward through the time. He hated feeling this helpless, this useless. He was used to being in control, to making things happen. But this was bigger than him, bigger than his resources. He was at the mercy of the system, and it was driving him insane.

He mentally rehearsed the words he would use and the promises he would make. He would tell her that everything was being taken care of. He would tell her that he missed her, that he needed her. Most importantly, he would tell her he was ready to fight tooth and nail to get her home with him.

A sudden, sharp ping tore through his reverie. His breath hitched. He snatched up his phone, his heart hammering against his ribs. A message from Tanya:

"NYC Skyline Sketches. Sector 7, tomorrow 10:00 AM."

The message was terse and impersonal, but to Aarav, it was the most beautiful thing he had ever read. Relief washed over him, so potent it almost made him dizzy. Tomorrow. He would see her tomorrow.

A small smile, the first genuine one in days, touched his lips. While it wasn't the joyous reunion he had imagined, it was a start.

The air in the grand hall hummed with a low, reverent buzz. Navya, in her sunflower-yellow dress, trailed a step behind Kavya. Kavya, dressed in a comfortable, paint-splattered canvas jacket, moved with a quiet intensity, her dark eyes taking in every detail.

They had come to an art exhibition, a showcase of promising contemporary artists.

"Look at this one, Kav," Navya said, her voice a soft murmur, drawing her sister towards a towering abstract piece. Swirls of violent crimson and bruised purple battled across the canvas, punctuated by jagged shards of deep blue.

"What do you think it means?" Navya asked.

Kavya smiled a small, knowing smile.

"Mean? It doesn't necessarily mean anything, Dee. It feels. It's about emotion, about the raw, untamed energy within," She gestured with her hand. "Look at the brushstrokes, the sheer force of them. You can almost feel the artist's frustration, their passion."

Navya smiled, finally Kavya was getting back to normal.

They moved on, passing by delicate sculptures crafted from reclaimed wood, their surfaces whispering stories of forests and time; then to installations of woven metal, catching the light in dazzling displays of intricate geometry; and finally, to a series of haunting portraits, each face etched with a unique tale of joy and sorrow.

Suddenly, Navya felt Kavya grip her arm way too tightly. She turned to look at her. Kavya was looking at something across the room. She followed her gaze.

There, amidst the hushed whispers of art aficionados, stood Aarav, his shoulders stiff, his gaze a mix of guilt and defiance. Flanking him were Aryan and Avni, their faces flushed with excitement. Navya's breath hitched. Next to her, Kavya looked at the three in surprise and confusion,

"Bhabhi!!" they both squealed and ran to hug her.

Navya held them in an embrace, but her eyes were on Aarav. Why was he here? Did he come to torture them? Make their life hell here? But then, why did he bring Aryan and Avni with him?

"What...What are you doing here?" Navya's voice was barely a whisper, laced with a dangerous edge. Her eyes darted between Aarav and his siblings, the blood draining from her face.

"Surprise!"

The air in the room crackled, not with the boisterous laughter of their siblings but with a silent tension that only Aarav and Navya seemed to perceive.

Aryan and Avni devoured the delicious meal cooked by their Bhabhi. Kavya, though, couldn't make eye contact with the three Singhania siblings.

Aarav's eyes, dark, stormy grey, were locked on Navya. He hadn't seen her in weeks. Weeks that had felt like an eternity, each day a dull ache of longing. He watched the way the lamplight caught the gold in her hazel eyes, the slight tremor in the corner of her lips. He wanted to reach out, to trace the line of her jaw, to hold her hand, and never let go. He hoped she would understand the depth of the feelings that had taken root in his heart without actually confessing. Each breath he took was a silent plea. *Please, let me take you home. Let me tell you everything.*

Navya, however, was a tightly coiled spring, unable to let go. She met Aarav's gaze, her own eyes shimmering with a mixture of longing and fear. She recognized the intensity in his look, the unspoken promise that jangled between them. He was like a magnet and her heart was drawn to him, but her mind screamed at her to pull back. This silent gaze, this unspoken communication, was a language they both knew too well. It was beautiful, intoxicating, and utterly terrifying.

He had hurt her before, the scars remained sharp reminders of the vulnerability she had exposed. She wasn't ready to be hurt again, but more than her, and she couldn't let him hurt her sister. his eyes spoke differently though. They were filled with something she had never seen before, but Navya couldn't decipher exactly what. But what if his gaze was just fleeting, a temporary spark that would soon fade? What if this longing was a mirage, and what lay on the other side was more pain? She could feel the warmth of his gaze on her. *Why is he looking at me like that? What is he plotting?*

A sudden burst of laughter from their siblings pulled them back to reality. Aryan and Avni were laughing loudly, while Kavya had a faint smile. Aarav felt a sigh of relief as he watched them like that after weeks. But as soon as Kavya met his eyes, her smile dropped.

Navya, her breath catching in her throat, felt a chilling realization wash over her. He had a plan. And she, caught in the web of her own complicated feelings, had no idea if she was ready to face it. The fear and longing warred within her, leaving her trembling slightly, unsure of what the night held and where her heart was leading her. All she knew was that the silent gaze had been a turning point, and the unspoken conversation had just begun.

♡♡♡

THIRTY-EIGHT

TANGLED EMOTIONS

At night, Aarav entered Navya's room, his heart beating rapidly. He watched her standing near the window. He closed the door gently.

"Avni slept in Kavya's room with her," Aarav began, his voice a low rumble, "Aryan is sleeping on the sofa in the living room."

Navya turned to him, her eyes full of questions.

"What do you want, Aarav?"

"To take you back home," he sighed.

"That isn't-"

"That is our home, Navya!" he cut her off, but his voice was gentle. "And I want you back in our home."

"So, did you think bringing Aryan and Avni would make me more... pliable? Like some human shield, so I can't refuse whatever you want."

Aarav winced, his shoulders slumping.

"You really think that of me? They were missing you, and I couldn't leave them there alone," he said, shaking his head. "Not anymore."

Navya didn't say anything. She missed them, too.

"I am sorry, Navya."

This sorry was nothing in comparison to the list of things he had to apologize for, but Aarav felt it was a start. Navya realized that this apology was a genuine one. It had always been genuine. Whatever Aarav said, he had always meant it.

"I know," he whispered, his voice cracking slightly. "I know I have made a huge mistake. I messed up everything," He ran a hand through his hair, his frustration evident. "But trust me, I would never do what you are afraid of today. I will never hurt Kavya."

Navya raised her gaze, waiting for him to continue.

"Or send her to jail," He swallowed hard. "I promise I won't do that. Let's go home."

A long silence fell between them, the only sound the distant chirping of crickets and the rustle of leaves in the light breeze. Navya's arms loosened.

"But you hated me, Aarav," she said, her voice low, almost a whisper. "Just because you thought I was behind the accident, and now, when you know it was Kavya, you would do nothing about it? Right. You'll just... forgive and forget? Is that it? You'll let Kavya get away with it. Do you really think I would believe that?"

"I... I know you don't trust me. And after everything, I can't blame you."

"Trust isn't something you can demand, Aarav."

"I was wrong. About everything," Aarav took a step towards her.

Navya looked into his eyes, searching for any lie, but she couldn't find any.

"I promise!" He insisted with a raw desperation. "I swear, Navya. I won't... I won't do anything to her," The words felt hollow even to his own ears. How could he possibly make her believe him after the hell he had put her through?

Navya's eyes narrowed, scrutinizing him with suspicion.

"You say that now, Aarav. But how can I believe you? I have faced your wrath. Maybe this is all another game," She walked closer to him, her small frame radiating a fierce protectiveness. "Don't think you can touch Kavya. Don't even think about it. You have taken enough from my life."

"Navya, please," Aarav pleaded, his voice thick with emotion. "I just want you to understand. I am not the monster you think I am."

Navya took a deep breath, the fight leaving her for a moment, and being replaced by weariness.

"I don't know what you are," She walked past him. "But I can tell you one thing. Kavya will not be a victim in your cruel game."

She walked towards the door, stopping with her hand on the handle.

"Maybe I can forgive you for what you did to me, Aarav, but I am not going to let you hurt my sister. Just stay away from her." She then walked away, leaving Aarav alone to face the consequences of his actions,a silent testament to the depth of the damage he had inflicted, the painful truth that even with the truth uncovered, some wounds might never heal.

The crisp New York air, a welcome change from the humid Indian climate, swirled around them as they stood at the foot of the bridge. Aarav shifted from one foot to the other, his gaze darting between the towering stone pillars and Navya, who was meticulously adjusting her scarf.

It was a journey for him to take his wife back into his life, but for Aryan and Avni, it was a family trip. They had convinced Navya to join them on a sightseeing trip, and here they were, at the Brooklyn Bridge, stealing glances at each other.

Aryan clapped his hands together.

"Guys, picture time! Let's get a groupfie with the bridge in the background."

Avni agreed and wrapped her hand around Navya, ready to pose. Kavya, however, seemed to shrink into herself, her eyes darting nervously towards Aarav whenever he moved. She had barely spoken a word since they met, her usual bubbly personality replaced by a quiet unease. Navya gave her sister a subtle nudge, a silent encouragement.

As Aryan organized them for the photo, Navya found herself sandwiched between Avni and Aarav. For a fraction of a second, their arms brushed. It was a fleeting contact, but a current seemed to run through her. She quickly moved, creating a small gap between them. Aarav, she noticed, had a similar, startled look on his face.

The photos were taken with awkward smiles plastered across their faces.

"Okay," Avni declared, "Let's walk across. I heard the views are amazing."

The walk across the bridge was a microcosm of their entire situation. The group progressed in a somewhat disjointed fashion. Aryan, with his easy charm, tried to engage everyone while Avni was busy snapping photos. Kavya walked slightly behind Navya, almost as if using her as a shield from Aarav. And Navya? She found herself swinging between wanting to give Aarav space and a strange, unavoidable pull to him.

Aarav, for his part, mirrored her hesitance. He kept a respectful distance, but his eyes frequently sought hers. He had caught her gaze, a flicker of something hopeful in his expression, and then quickly looked away. Navya noticed a sadness in his eyes that hadn't been there before. It was different from the arrogance that had fueled their arguments all the time.

Halfway across, they stopped to admire the cityscape, the Manhattan skyline glittering in the afternoon sun. As Aryan and Avni debated the merits of different buildings, Navya found herself momentarily alone with Aarav by the railing.

"It's beautiful," Aarav said softly, his voice barely audible over the wind.

Navya nodded, her throat suddenly tight.

He continued, "I... I wanted to say...I am glad you came. I know it must be difficult."

She looked at him, her eyes searching his.

"It is," she admitted, choosing her words carefully. "But... I couldn't break their hearts."

Before he could respond, Kavya, who had been watching them from a distance, suddenly called out, "Dee, are you coming? They are already going ahead," There was an edge of panic in her voice.

Navya's gaze shifted to her sister, and she saw the slight tremor in her hands. She gave Aarav a fleeting but reassuring look.

"I have to go."

He nodded, understanding. The brief moment of connection was broken and replaced by the reality of their fragile situation. Even amidst the stunning backdrop of New York City, their path to reconciliation was proving to be a winding one, filled with hurdles, both internal and external. The bridges they needed to cross were not just made of stone and steel but of months of hurt and unspoken truths. And it would take more than a sightseeing trip to mend what had been broken.

THIRTY-NINE

A Bridge Across the Chasm?

The living room was filled in the quiet of a late afternoon. Dust motes danced in the slanting sunlight, illuminating the untouched surfaces. Kavya sat on the edge of the sofa, her gaze fixed on a book. Aarav had been watching her for the last few minutes, a knot of worry tightening in his chest. Navya was away for some work. It was the right time, he thought.

He took a deep breath and walked over, settling a respectful distance away on the armchair.

"Kavya," he began, his voice soft, almost hesitant, not wanting to shatter the fragile silence.

She didn't look up, but he saw her hand tremble slightly.

"Yes," she acknowledged him, her voice barely a whisper.

He knew he had to push gently but firmly.

"I have been... I have been wanting to talk to you. But Navya told me to stay away from you."

She finally lifted her eyes, her face etched with a mixture of apprehension and guilt. Aarav knew that look well. It haunted her almost as much as the memory of that day haunted him.

"About?" she asked, her voice still strained.

"About... everything," he replied, his gaze unwavering. "About what happened."

Kavya flinched. She placed her cup on the small table with a clatter, the sound reverberating in the quiet room. She finally met his gaze, her eyes wide and vulnerable.

"Jiju, please," she whispered, her voice cracking. "I... I don't want to talk about it."

Aarav understood that fear, understood the urge to bury the past deep. But he knew that real healing couldn't happen without acknowledging the pain. He leaned forward, his voice earnest.

"Kavya, I know. I know it's hard. But I need you to understand something. I need you to hear me."

Tears welled in her eyes, threatening to spill.

"What?" she breathed.

He closed the distance between them, kneeling before her, his eyes reaching for hers.

"I don't blame you, Kavya. Not even a little bit," His voice was low, filled with the weight of years of silent understanding. "I know it was an accident, a terrible, heartrending accident. You were just fifteen, a kid. You didn't intend for any of it to happen."

Her breath hitched, and a tear finally escaped, tracing a path down her cheek.

"But... but it was me," she cried, her voice thick with emotion. "If I hadn't... If I hadn't that night-"

He took her hands in his, his thumbs gently stroking her skin.

"Don't," he cut her off gently. "Don't do it to yourself." He looked into her eyes. "I have spent years... years wrestling with the pain, with the loss and the 'what ifs.' And I have finally realized... lashing out at you, and holding you responsible... it wouldn't bring them back. It wouldn't make the pain go away. It would just... add another layer of hurt. I have made this mistake once, not again."

The tears now flowed freely, blurring her vision. She reached out a hand and touched his cheek with trembling fingers.

"You... you really don't..."

Aarav nodded, his voice thick with emotion.

"Never. You're my family, Kavya. And holding onto this... this unspoken pain between us... It's tearing us apart."

A sob tore through her, and she launched herself forward, burying her face against his chest. He wrapped his arms tightly around her, letting her cry, letting her release the years of unspoken grief and guilt. He felt his own tears begin to fall, mixing with hers as he hugged her close.

"I am so sorry, Jiju," she choked between sobs. "I had almost forgotten the accident. It was that day when you mentioned it that I remembered. If I had known it was your parents, I would have told you myself. I am sorry."

"Shhh," he murmured, stoking her hair. "It's okay. It's going to be okay."

They stayed like that for what felt like a long time, the tears flowing, the unspoken words finally finding their release. The weight of unspoken tension began to ease like a slow, painful exhale finally let go.

Navya pushed open the front door, worried. She had been at a particularly grueling client meeting, but she was worried about Kavya, who was still hesitant to face Aarav and Aarav because she didn't trust his anger. But the scene that unfolded before her as she arrived home made her heart clench with a nameless emotion.

Aarav was sprawled across the plush rug in the living room. His usually serious brow was furrowed, not in his characteristic concentration, but in exaggerated annoyance. He was waving a red 'Reverse' card in the air, his gaze fixed on his younger brother, who was leaning back against the couch, a smug grin plastered across his face.

"You can't skip me twice in a row!" Aarav protested, his voice laced with a mock indignation that rarely surfaced.

"Technically, I can," Aryan retorted, his grin widening as he pointed towards Avni, their younger sister, who sat beside him, her face beaming with mischievous glee. "I played a skip, then Avni played a skip. Rules say we can. Face it, Bhai! You're just bad at UNO."

Navya's eyes then flickered to the other side of the rug. Kavya laughed, a delicate sound that she had yearned to hear. She placed her hand lightly on Aarav's arm, her eyes sparkling with amusement.

"Relax, Jiju. It's just a game."

It was that hand, that light touch, that brought amusement to her face. Kavya and Aarav? Kavya had been too distant with Aarav, getting nervous around him. And Aarav, Navya thought he would say hurtful words to her. But here they were, practically conspirators in a game of UNO, a shared laughter bubbling between them. It was a sight that felt... off, like a misaligned jigsaw puzzle piece that refused to fit into the overall picture.

"See, Bhai? Even Kavya agrees. You need to chill," Aryan quipped, earning a glare from his brother.

"You two are ganging up on me!" Aarav declared, turning to Kavya with an almost pleading look. "Tell them, Kavya, tell them I am right."

Kavya chuckled again, a sweet, melodic sound that made Navya's smile widen.

"Honestly, Jiju, you're being a bit dramatic." She said, pushing him playfully. 'But I think, technically, Aryan is right."

Aarav's dramatic indignation dissolved into a reluctant smile, and he threw his hands up in mock surrender.

"Fine, fine. I am outnumbered."

The playful quarrel continued, the cards slapped down with practiced ease, the laughter bouncing off the walls. Navya stood unnoticed at the doorway, watching the strange dynamics play before her. Her mind raced, trying to make sense of it all.

Aryan and Avni were usually the inseparable duo, always scheming together. Aarav, with his logical and organized mind, was usually the voice of reason, even in games. And Kavya, the quiet observer, was now the center of this unexpected alliance. It was as if the siblings had swapped personalities, and Kavya had suddenly been given a role she had never played before.

Taking a deep breath, she cleared her throat.

"Hey, everyone," she announced. Everyone turned, their laughter and playful banter momentarily suspended.

Then, a bright smile lightened up their face.

"Bhabhi! You are back!" Avni beamed at her sister-in-law.

Aarav couldn't help but smile. He looked at Navya, taking in her tired but beautiful features. This must have been what a person lost in a desert must feel like after looking at water. Content.

FORTY

ECHOES FADE, PROMISES BLOOM

Aarav stood nervously at the entrance of Navya's room, his heart pounding in his chest. He had planned this moment for weeks, rehearsing his words and preparing his heart.

Navya sat curled on the edge of the sofa, her eyes red-rimmed, a single tear tracing a path down her cheek. The vibrant floral cushions were a stark contrast to the storm brewing within her. Aarav walked to stand in front of her, his hands clenched, his usual confident demeanor replaced with nervousness.

"Navya," he called her with all the warmth he had in his voice.

"What do you want from me, Aarav?" she asked without looking at him. "What game are you planning?"

Aarav frowned, confused.

"Game?"

"Kavya is also getting better. If you have genuinely forgiven her, then thank you so much. I think you should go back to India with the kids now."

Aarav's heartbeat stopped for a moment.

"If you want me to go back, then I will," He sat in front of her. "But I want to go back, with you. Please come with me."

"Why?" She finally looked at him. "You don't need me. You have everything that you want. And why the hell did you come here? Oh yes, because Aryan and Avni missed me. I'll convince them that this is how it is going to be. They won't ask to meet me, so please go back."

He opened his mouth to speak when Navya interrupted, her brow furrowed, her eyes sharp and accusatory.

"Don't you dare start with your excuses," Navya interrupted, her eyes flashing. "I know that you meet Samaira behind my back."

Aarav closed his eyes briefly, willing his heart to slow its frantic pace.

"Navya, it wasn't like that."

"Then what was it like, Aarav?" She stood up as her voice rose, the quiet accusation turning into a torrent of emotion. "What was it that you had to keep it a secret? You couldn't tell me about meeting her?"

He moved closer, his hand reaching towards hers but hesitating.

"Navya, please... It's just... it's not what you think."

Navya shook her head, more tears escaping.

"I saw you. I saw you both at the restaurant that day. You looked...comfortable. Like you were having your best time, The time I long for," She choked back a sob, her shoulders trembling. "Then that night, you left me to meet her... I heard you talking on the phone with her. You always wanted her in your life... you are going back to her. You never cared for me. All you want is...."

Before she could complete it, she felt Aarav pulling her into his arms. She stopped, shocked. Aarav closed his eyes, gripping her in his arms. Navya resisted and tried to move away, but he didn't let her go. Eventually, she melted in his arms.

"Don't make it more difficult for me, Aarav," she muttered, cocooned in his arms. "Please go back."

"I know I have been a bad husband," he admitted. "We both believed in a second chance, didn't we?"

Navya broke the embrace and looked at him.

"But you were always a great wife," he said, his voice barely above a whisper. "The way you care for my siblings, the way you organize the house, the quiet strength you possess. I... I was so busy being the man I thought I was supposed to be that I didn't see the woman you actually are."

Tears welled in Navya's eyes again.

"Aarav..." her voice wavered, the emotions she had held back finally pushing past her defenses.

He squeezed her hand gently, his gaze intent, searching.

"I know I haven't given you any reason to believe me, but I want to change that, Navya. I want to be better. I want you and me to be us."

He wrapped his hand around her waist and pulled her closer, keeping his forehead on hers.

"I love you, Navya," he confessed. "You are the most incredible woman I have ever met. You make me want to be a better man."

Navya's heart hammered against her ribs, hearing the confession.

She suddenly felt like the protagonist of a romance novel. Aarav, whose every glance felt like a dagger to her emotions, had just told her, with those serious, devastatingly handsome eyes, that he loved her. But her life wasn't a romance novel. It was a carefully choreographed dance of polite smiles, shared meals in comfortable silence, and a constant ache in her heart.

She had left the hope of Aarav loving her long back. But now, hearing him confess his love, she couldn't find a single word to say, not even a whisper. He loved her? Her Aarav loved her? The possibility was so overwhelming, so unbelievably perfect, that for a moment, she was lost and was floating somewhere between reality and a dream she dared not wake from. This wasn't how things were supposed to be. Or was it?

"But... you..."

Aarav gently cupped her face.

"Let me explain about Samaira."

Navya nodded slowly, her gaze still locked on his.

He took a deep breath.

"You already know she had decided to divorce her husband. "Navya nodded. "Her husband had lost his job, so I reached out to her. I didn't want her to make a wrong decision regarding this issue. She was my friend first, after all. I just wanted to help. I couldn't stand seeing someone struggling like that."

Navya frowned.

"Help how?"

"I got Rohan a job at my company. I didn't want to make a big thing out of it, you know? It was just... a good deed, Navya. They are together now," He looked at her, his eyes pleading for her to understand. "I wanted to fix the situation without bragging or drawing attention to myself. I didn't even tell Megha about it. I know I should have told you, but I was scared... scared of how it might look. Scared something like this might... happen."

Navya stared at him, processing his words. Her anger started to recede, replaced by a confused mix of emotions: disbelief, relief, and a strange pang of guilt.

"You..." she started, her voice soft. "You helped Rohan get a job so that he and Samaira would get back together?"

Aarav nodded, his gaze sincere.

"Yes. That's all I was doing. Rohan has already joined," He brushed a stray strand of hair from her face. "Navya, please believe me. There is no one else. It's only you."

A slow smile touched Navya's lips, the first genuine one in what felt like a lifetime. She reached out, taking his hand and intertwining their fingers, and leaning in to press her forehead against his. The storm had finally subsided, leaving behind a quiet calm, the promise of a new dawn.

She looked at him, her eyes reflecting the warmth of the sunset.

"I love you, Aarav. I have for a long time."

Aarav took a deep breath, his hands trembling slightly.

He moved closer, making her heart beat rapidly. For the first time since their marriage, the distance between them, both physical and emotional, seemed to shrink, replaced by a hesitant intimacy.

He turned her chin gently with his fingers, forcing her to meet his gaze. His eyes, usually sharp and distant, were now filled with love. Navya gasped.

Slowly, he leaned in, his gaze lingering on her lips for a moment before he finally closed the distance. His lips brushed hers in a tender yet intense kiss. It took a moment for Navya to register what was happening, but soon her resistance melted away, and she found herself responding, her hands threading through his hair.

The world around them seemed to blur as the kiss deepened, their emotions pouring out in a whirlwind of passion and need. Aarav's heart raced, and he pulled her closer, never wanting this moment to end. Navya's doubts and fears faded, and she felt a deep connection, a bond that went beyond words.

When the two broke apart, Navya's breath was ragged, and her eyes were wide with surprise and hope.

"I love you too, Navya. Please never give up on us. I promise to be here for you, to support you, and to help you heal. And I promise to never take you for granted again."

Navya's eyes glistened with unshed tears, but her smile was radiant.

"I promise the same. We'll heal, and we'll grow, and we'll find our way back to each other. I promise we'll never give up on each other."

Aarav held her tighter.

"I'll do everything in my power to make you happy. To make us happy. I need you to trust me, to let me in."

Navya's eyes met his, and she nodded.

"I trust you, Aarav. I trust us. And I'll be here for you every step of the way."

The future was uncertain, but they were ready to face it together, with the promise of healing and a new beginning guiding them forward.

Epilogue I

The warm glow of the setting sun painted the skyline in hues of orange and gold, a familiar backdrop to the rooftop party that Navya and Aarav were hosting. Laughter, the clinking of glasses, and the gentle hum of conversation filled the air – a far cry from the tense silences and unspoken resentments that had once plagued their marriage. The rollercoaster had finally reached a steady, joyous climb.

Navya, in a flowing copper sulfate dress of her own design, moved effortlessly through the crowd, a radiant smile on her face. Her brand, "NK Designs," had grown, her unique creations gracing the covers of fashion magazines. Tonight, especially, she felt an immense sense of accomplishment and, more importantly, a deep resonance of love. She caught Aarav's eye across the throng. He stood taller than most, his architect's frame relaxed yet confident, a small smile playing on his lips as he spoke with a client about his latest building design. His eyes held that same quiet intensity she had loved, lost, and found again.

Their journey from a broken arranged marriage to this point had been nothing short of a miracle. They had learned to communicate, to truly see each other, not as the people their families had chosen, but as individuals with dreams and flaws. The painful separations had carved out a more profound understanding. Their love was like any great work of art, it had been painstakingly crafted, layer by layer, through trials that had seemed insurmountable. Now, everything clicked.

"Looking good, sis! This party is a total hit," Kavya approached with a tray of appetizers, her eyes sparkling with a mix of mischief and excitement.

"Thank you so much. You are on time, but where is your business partner?" Navya asked, scanning her eyes through the hall.

"He didn't tell you? He has invited someone special. He must be waiting for her near the gate."

The sisters giggled.

Kavya, now a businesswoman, had found her stride as the operations whiz behind Aryan's burgeoning tech startup called "ConnectSphere." They made an excellent team, Kavya handling the logistics and finance while Aryan focused on innovation and marketing. However, her love for art was still a part of her, and she would still sketch when she could find the time.

And then, they saw Aryan, walking hand in hand with Khushi, his ever-efficient and now smitten secretary. She was invited to a family function for the first time.

"Look at them," Kavya whispered to Navya. "They are practically glowing. I never thought I would see the day when Aryan actually fell in love with someone who wasn't a spreadsheet."

Navya chuckled.

"He's changed, hasn't he? And you have finally found someone who appreciates your organized chaos," She nudged her shoulder against Kavya's.

"Yeah," Kavya blushed. "But where is he?"

She looked around the hall for her fiancé.

"I didn't invite him," Navya said in a plain tone

Kavya's head turned to look at her in shock.

"Why?"

"Navya crossed her arms.

"Last week, when, I planned a get-together at home, he didn't show up."

"Dee," Kavya sighed. "You know he had a last-minute work thing."

Navya raised a perfectly sculpted eyebrow.

"A 'work thing'? Interesting. Two months engaged, and already he is bailing on your family get-together. Just saying," Navya suppressed a smile.

"He is probably just overwhelmed," Kavya defended.

She knew Navya was just teasing, but it still stung a little. He was a little overwhelming... in the best way possible. His constant pampering sometimes felt like being wrapped in a warm, fuzzy blanket, and sometimes Kavya just needed a little room to breathe.

As if the universe had decided to play a prank, a familiar, deep voice cut through the playful jabber.

"Overwhelmed, am I? Well, I wouldn't want to miss a party, especially when my beautiful fiancé looks the most beautiful."

Kavya's heart skipped a beat. She turned sharply, and there he was. Sahil. His dark eyes sparkling with amusement, a bouquet of her favorite white lilies and pink roses held in his hand. He was dressed in a dark blue 3-piece suit, and his smile was the one that always made her knees go weak.

Kavya's cheeks flushed crimson.

"You are early!" Navya said in an accusatory tone.

"Yeah, Bhabhi," he rolled his eyes. "I couldn't have you tease my fiancée, could I?"

They both burst out laughing.

He presented her with the bouquet. The sweet fragrance filled Kavya's nostrils, and she took it with trembling hands, her blush deepening. She felt like a heroine in one of the Bollywood movies she adored.

"Thank you," she whispered, a smile playing on her lips.

Sahil leaned closer, his breath tickling her ear. Pulling her closer by her shoulder, he gently placed a soft kiss on her forehead.

"Look at you two," Aryan joined in, Khushi to his side. "Is the hashtag #LogisticsQueenInLove going to trend, Kavya?"

Kavya rolled her eyes, a familiar teasing chuckle escaping her lips.

"Very funny. As if #BossInLove is not trending yet."

"I wish!" Aryan looked at Khushi, who blushed profusely.

"And for your information," Kavya shot. "Someone needs to keep an eye on the budget,"

"Right, right, the budget that keeps funding my crazy ideas. I guess you are my rock, and you complain the least, you know," Aryan winked at Kavya.

They had forged an unbreakable bond during the last year, their personalities clashing and complementing. Their company was thriving. Their best-friendship was now a regular feature of all the family conversations.

Sahil chuckled, shaking his head at their antics.

"You two are worse than a married couple," he quipped.

"Married couples are worse than us!" Kavya and Aryan replied simultaneously, then looked at each other and burst out laughing.

"Hey!" Aarav, looking undeniably handsome, joined, a playful glint in his dark eyes. "What's so funny that I am missing out on?"

Navya leaned over to her husband, her eyes sparkling.

"You could never miss any moment in my life."

Aarav wrapped his arm around her waist, pulling her close.

"I would never," He glanced at his brother, then at Khushi, her laughter echoing.

Just as Aarav was about to address her, a familiar chime echoed from his phone. He glanced at the screen, and a wide grin spread across his face.

"Hold up everyone. Avni's calling!"

They erupted in excited murmurs. Avni was miles away in the US, pursuing her master's, and they hadn't seen her in almost a year. Aarav quickly answered the video call, his face filling the screen.

Avni's smiling face, a bit pixelated but undeniably glowing, appeared on the screen.

"Happy Anniversary!" she exclaimed, her voice ringing with genuine joy. The backdrop behind her was a blurry cityscape at twilight.

"Avni! Look at you, you look amazing," Navya said, her eyes filled with affection. She moved closer to the phone. "We miss you."

"I miss you guys, too," Avni replied. "But you know I have exams next month, and the classes are intense this week. But honestly, seeing you all feels like a breath of fresh air," Her smile shifted, becoming a little wistful. "But I wish I could be there with you tonight."

"You are going to make us proud, Avni," Navya said sincerely, trying to lighten her mood. "There are compromises you would have to make."

"And we're saving a slice of cake with your name on it," Aryan added, playfully winking at the camera.

"Okay, give me the phone now, and you guys cut the cake," Kavya said, taking the phone from Aarav's hand.

A chorus of agreement echoed around them. The tiered confection, a masterpiece of white frosting and delicate sugar roses, sat patiently on a small table. It was a testament to their five years together, a sweet symbol of their enduring love. Yet, both Aarav and Navya exchanged hesitant glances.

Navya squeezed Aarav's hand, silently communicating with their eyes.

"Cutting cake can wait," Aarav looked at Navya, who nodded.

"But why, beta?" Rajesh Oberoi asked as he walked towards them with his wife.

"Papa, please." His voice, pleading. "We are waiting for someone."

After Aarav and Navya had sorted out their differences, for a couple of years, dinners at her parents' house had been polite, stilted affairs. Aarav had maintained a respectful distance, addressing them as "Aunty" and "Uncle". Navya remembered the day he finally called them 'Maa' and 'Papa.' It had been Diwali, the festival of lights, a symbol of hope and new beginnings. Standing amidst the flickering *diyas*, surrounded by the family, the words had just tumbled out, raw and choked with emotion. The tears that followed were a mixture of grief, relief, and an unexpected sense of peace.

"Of course," Anjali said smiling. "But when are they reaching?"

"Just a little longer, Maa." Aarav answered while his eyes scanned the entrance.

♡♡♡

Epilogue Ii

“Just a little longer, Maa." Aarav answered while his eyes scanned the entrance. They had been waiting for two more people.

A few more calls of "Cake! Cake!" rose from the crowd, causing Aarav to chuckle nervously.

"Patience, everyone," he called out, his voice laced with a hint of the anticipation he was trying to mask. "We have very special guests... that we're waiting for."

Just as another impatient "Aarav! It's been an hour" rose from the crowd, a commotion rippled through the gathering near the entrance. Heads turned, conversations died down, and a collective murmur filled the air. And then, they appeared.

Megha, radiant in a flowing emerald green dress, her dark hair cascading down her shoulders, walked into the hall, her hand intertwined with her husband, Mohit. A collective cheer erupted as soon as she was spotted. Megha's smile was wide and warm, crinkling the corner of her eyes, as she scanned the space for Aarav and Navya.

Aarav's face lit up, his patience rewarded. He released a sigh, a mixture of relief and pure joy. Navya's eyes sparkled with tears as she struggled to hold back. They moved forward, not toward the cake, but towards Megha.

"Megha!" Navya cried, pulling her into a tight hug as soon as she was within reach. Aarav embraced Mohit, patting him on the back with genuine warmth.

"We thought you might be lost in traffic!" Aarav joked, his voice full of affection.

Megha laughed, a musical sound that swept through the crowd.

"We would never miss this," she said, her eyes sparkling. "Happy anniversary, you two. So sorry we were late; Mohit was stuck in a conference call."

Mohit raised a hand in mock apology; "The joys of being a businessman."

With Megha and her husband now present, the party truly felt complete. Aarav and Navya exchanged a look, their eyes mirroring each other's elation.

"Alright, everyone," Navya called out, her voice vibrant with happiness. "Let's cut this cake!"

A spontaneous cheer went up as everyone surged around the table, their faces beaming. Megha and Mohit arrived, completing the circle of loved ones around Aarav and Navya. They knew at that moment that the love they shared was not just between them but extended outwards, encompassing friendship, support, and the shared joy of celebrating life's precious moments.

Hours later, standing separated from the crowd, Aarav and Navya looked at their family. Aryan looked slightly flushed next to Khushi; Kavya was practically radiating happiness beside her Sahil; and Megha still had that newlywed glow, even after three years of her marriage, subtly holding Mohit's hand.

Aarav leaned in, his forehead resting against his wife.

"We made it, Navya," he whispered, his voice thick with emotion.

"We did, Aarav," she replied, her voice soft.

"I can't believe you guys are still finding corners away in the party! “Megha quipped walking towards them, with Mohit. "It's been five years after all!"

"Still less to adore your wife. I still can't thank her enough for coming into my life!" Aarav grinned, grabbing a glass of champagne from a passing waiter. "And now that I'm a seasoned pro – I feel I must pass on some hard-earned wisdom. Especially to the younger generation," He waggled a teasing finger at Aryan.

Aryan, already looking slightly uncomfortable, groaned.

"Oh god, here we go," He slipped an arm around Khushi, who offered a polite but slightly nervous smile.

"The key to a successful relationship," Aarav continued, "Is communication. Not just talking, but listening. Really listening. See how Navya's eyes sparkle when I talk about my work? Okay, maybe not always, but at least she pretends to care!" He winked at Navya, earning a playful shove from her.

"Aarav!" Navya laughed, then looked at Aryan and Khushi. "He's right though, communication is key. It's not always easy, but it's worth the effort."

"And," Aarav picked up the thread. "Don't be afraid to be vulnerable, to show your true selves to each other. No facades, okay?" He looked intently at Aryan, who managed a nod. "And a little grand gesture now and then doesn't hurt either. Flowers, a handwritten note..." He glanced at Navya who smiled indulgently.

He then turned his attention to Kavya and Sahil.

"You two, the engaged ones! Marriage is not just a fairytale; it takes work. But it's the most rewarding work you'll ever do. You two are pretty perfect together if you both are as happy as you are right now," he playfully jabbed Sahil on the arm.

"We know, we know," Sahil said, beaming at Kavya. "We're taking notes, Bhai.'

Finally, Aarav's gaze landed on Megha and Mohit.

"Married for three years already, but after the craziness dies down, remember to keep the spark alive. Never stop dating each other, never stop laughing together."

Mohit, completely smitten with Megha, nodded enthusiastically.

"Definitely!"

"And most importantly," Aarav concluded, his tone softening, "Never forget what brought you together in the first place. Remember that spark, that initial connection. Nurture it, cherish it, and never stop choosing each other. Find a language to sort out your conflicts, make it your love language."

The group was silent for a moment, absorbing Aarav's unexpected sermon.

Navya, with a fond smile, wrapped her arm around Aarav's waist.

Aarav wrapped his arm around Navya, drawing her closer. "Speaking of love languages, this party is my way of saying thank you, to you, to us, and to everyone who believed in us," he said, his voice thick with emotion. He looked at Megha who nodded her head at the hidden acknowledgement.

Aarav pressed a soft kiss on the top of Navya's head.

Their journey hadn't been easy. There were still moments of frustration, clashing personalities, and the occasional flare-up. But they had learned the language of compromise, the art of forgiveness, and the sheer determination to fight for their love, not against each other. They had learned that a strong foundation isn't built on avoiding conflict but on navigating it together.

Five years. Five years of painstakingly rebuilding trust, of learning to communicate beyond the initial hurt and anger. Five years of showing the world that second chances, even in the spotlight, were possible but incredibly beautiful.

Their Instagram feed, once a curated collection of carefully posed images, now showcased a more authentic narrative. Pictures of messy family dinners, Aarav helping Navya cook, Navya pressing his head after a tiring day, candid shots of them laughing until their sides hurt. Their followers, initially captivated by the drama, had grown to admire their resilience, their unwavering commitment, and the quiet strength in their shared glances.

Their story wasn't a fairytale, not a seamless progression from heartbreak to happily ever after. It was a testament to the messy, unpredictable, gloriously imperfect nature of love. It was a reminder that even the most fractured pieces could be painstakingly reassembled, stronger, and more beautiful than before, a mosaic of scars and triumphs, a testament to a love that had survived its own destruction. And as the night deepened, they sat there, hand in hand, two architects of their own destiny, their love story a masterpiece still unfolding, one brushstroke at a time.

www.ingramcontent.com/pod-product-compliance
Lightning Source LLC
LaVergne TN
LVHW041205150826
845673LV00001B/296

* 9 7 9 8 8 9 7 2 4 4 3 0 0 *